Primal Desires: Mating Season is published by:

Kindle Direct Publishing

ISBN: 9781094687919

First Printing: February 2014

Printed in the United States of America

Dear Readers,

I apologize about the name change of the series, but it had to be done. What you once knew as 'Animal Instincts: The Hunt,' is now 'Primal Desires: The Hunt Begins.' The first book of this series.

I hope you enjoy reading 'Mating Season,' as much as I enjoyed writing it. And thank you so much for reading my books. Be on the lookout for my third novel in the 'Primal Desires,' series titled: 'Primal Desires: Cravings.'

Jamie

This book is dedicated to Lacey D. Carr

"My Father"

Primal Desires

Mating Season

Jamie

Preface

Tatum..............

There is a lesson to be learned when growing up. Too bad it had to be *me* who learned it the hard way.

Since the night my mother died, my motto had been, 'strive to always be better than my father.' Recently I discovered that I'm worse. The only thing Motif is at fault for is being who he is. Everyone knew what type of man he was and the people on this island had no other choice but to accept him as their Chief. I guess that's why Jameria was so eager to go back to the States. You get to change leaders every 4 to 8 years. Here, on the island our bloodline rules.

When my grandfather, the late Vilmander Flask looked upon his one and only heir while covering his beautiful wife's face after she took her last breath, he was buoyed beyond belief to find he had a daughter. The first ever in our history. His wife gave him a gift that he would cherished to his dying day. He named his precious daughter Ky. Short for (Keeping You). Ky made history by being the first female to be born of a Chief. Growing up as Mistress was a safe, secure, fun, and exciting life. But it also had its drawbacks. Uncle Demarcus and my mom grew up together.

pack will be behind me no matter what, I still see the hurt in their eyes, knowing we won't be going to the States after all.

Jameria had bought a house in Boston. We were *finally* going to attend college. Uncle Demarcus and Rubea' would've been with us as guardians for the rest still attending high school for the first time in our lives. Those were Jameria plans, to be our age.

My plans was to keep her as close by my side as possible. Her eggs and my seed was just the beginning of what I had in mind, and if I had told her those plans she would've left me for sure. That is what I could not accept, so I kept my plans to myself and followed through to the end. But, in the process I manage to enslave us all, because just like my mother before me, I let Motif in my head.

I'm a fuck up.

Jameria almost killing Noonie, was an interesting site, but tonight ended being one of the strangest nights of my life. And all of it is my fault. I should have gotten the full story leading up to Jameria's birth. But it was what I wanted and what I still want.

Jameria slept in my arms after the ass whipping she gave. She still hasn't answered my question about marriage, but at least she wasn't trying to kill me anymore.

As I was dozing, two things happened. I pulled Jameria close, spooning her from behind, with my hand resting on her still flat belly. I heard a hiss in the quiet room. I let the moonlight be my guide, staring directly into her face, finding her sound asleep. Not letting it cross my mind a second time, I got back into my comfort zone, determined to let the Sandman do his thing. I let my mind wonder back to the things I've done, and the things I have left to do. Not realizing I was drifting off in dreamland, I found myself in the middle of a lush field. The dream was so vivid.

My son was born, but instead of one, it was two identical faces.

They were beautiful.

Long shiny black hair floated behind them as they ran and played. Their golden skin glistening in the sun, as they try to best each other. Then the scene changed and they were surrounded by wolves and snakes of all shapes and sizes. Not aggressively, but protecting.

A dark shadow rose above their young heads. A swarm of locusts, wasps, mantises, scorpions, and spiders were moving in on them from all directions. Both boys got into aggressive crouches. Moving with lightning speed, both flipped high in the air, landing on the backs of green scaled anacondas. Gaboon vipers slithered up their slender arms. The insects' descended......

My eyes snapped opened, but they were still cloaked in darkness.

Then realization hit.

We were covered in snakes.

I could hear them hissing. Feel them gliding over our bodies, as in a sensual caress. Jameria was still in my arms

Tatum immediately wrapped both of his arms around her torso. Realizing what he was doing, Kelanie joined him by sandwiching our Mistress between them and wrapping her slender arms around her also. Soon everyone caught on to what was wrong.Shit!!!! The baby was controlling the snakes.............A story from long ago, told by Pat Ann Beau. Jameria's grandmother. A story that still gives me nightmares to this day.

Our entire pack was holding onto our Mistress, blocking the baby from the snakes. With both arms reaching for the sky, she let out a long menacing hiss. Her enormous anacondas came from the forest and surrounded our group. Beautiful shades of blue, green, black, the smallest one being at least 20 feet long, dotted in yellow. Their heads high above the palace, hissing right along with Jameria. We could feel her soft frame quivering. We saw the invading snakes, scattering in different directions, overlapping each other to get as far away from the palace as possible. Jameria snakes, in one swift motion, one huge reptile after the next slithered from one end of the palace to the other before they roam passed us, hissing their way through.

Jameria lowered her arms and announced, "All clean."

We all stood slowly, releasing our embrace from her body.

"Are you alright," Tatum whispered, holding her close, with his forehead against hers.

"What just happened? I thought you couldn't be around snakes until *after* you gave birth?" Cougar was pacing back and forward like a lioness in heat.

She didn't answer. Instead, Jameria stared at her arms confused as to why the young vipers' still refused to leave her body. "Meet me in my rooms in two hours. Boaz, Pierce, you and your mates stay in my bedroom and watch these things until after the Council meeting," she said, her gaze

lingering longer on Boaz. I've notice her doing that a lot, lately. The look is almost like she sees a totally different Boaz from the young handsome boy standing in front of us.

Instead of going back to my suite, I showered with Kelanie in hers.

"Has anything like this happened, while we were on the hunt?"

Kelanie was running her small fingers through my long hair scrubbing the soap out, while I ran my hands over every inch of her. Her cinnamon body, my playground. Fat ass, small waist, and can ride a dick like a cowboy on a bull.

"No, but for a whole week, Jameria had been locked in her room, refusing to see anyone. When you guys were due back, her suite door swung open and she had that same expression she had on her face the day she killed my bird. I knew it had something to do with Tatum, because the picture frame of the two of them on her mantel was smashed."

Dammit Tatum.

He can barely control himself. How the hell is he going to raise a kid that has the gift of controlling snakes? And, there is a possibility that he or she can control the wolves also.

Fuck! This is not what we need right now.

I tried to put my mind in a better place. I held my head under water, letting the suds drain down my back while Kelanie finished what she'd started earlier.

Jameria taught her well.

I watched my baby practice that entire night, trying to swallow a peeled banana whole. I was so proud when she got the whole thing down without gagging.

Now my dick felt like her last meal. Her lips soft, mouth hot and wet. She likes to call this her "preparation before intercourse."

Since I came back from our first hunt, Kelanie had never been the same again.

   We were sixteen at the time and our pack had just been deemed men. Noonie threw a party on the beach, but later that night Kelanie and I had our own *first* party. I bust her fat ass wide open the first time we had sex. I couldn't wait to get back to dig in that ass. It had tempted me for far too long. But that was then……this is now.

I pulled her up against the wall.

 "You hate having sex standing," she said kissing my neck.

 "Well, we wouldn't be in this position if I hadn't felt my *hard-on* refusing to *hold-on* and unload down your throat." I lick her soft lips. "That's not how I want to cum."

I entered her slowly, feeding her inches at a time. She wrapped her legs around my waist, pulling me in deeper. I grabbed two handfuls of her ass and remembered why I don't like having sex standing. Kelanie have such a beautiful ass, that it deserved to be admired at all times. Standing was not an option. I want to have a perfect view of the plump perfection. So I hurriedly cut off the shower and took her to the bed still connected.

And I took her hard and rough.

I tied her arms to the heavy oaked headboard, then lifting her legs and spreading them, I tied her ankles beside each arm gaining full access as I ate her sweet pussy and ass out like ice cream on a hot sunny day. I spread her pussy lips and let my tongue take a journey within her folds at a slow pace as I memorized every tingle, taste, and moan she gave me. I felt each of her orgasms between her quivering thighs, tasted her sweet nectar that's meant for me and only me.

After the last shiver left her body, I sat back on my hunches admiring the spectacular view. I love her in this position with her legs and arms spread wide like a butterfly spreading its wings. Sweet cream leaking from her slick folds. My erection was so hard, semen seeped from the head as I inched my way up her apple scented body. With her juices still coating my face, I shoved my tongue down her throat, and shoved my 11 inch pole in her twat, fucking her with no mercy. And she matched every thrust with a hunger.

She clenched me, thrust her pussy at me, tried to suck my fucking tongue down her throat, pulling hard against the ties as I pushed her legs so far apart, the letter V came to mind.

I held her ass up as I slid my lower part under her, spreading my legs, so my knees won't be in contact with the head board. I let her anus glide down my rod slowly, until she was firmly seated in place. I could feel her suctioning me further in her cave. I placed both of my hands under each cheek and began bouncing that ass off my dick while nut shot out of her pussy in spurts, on my abdomen. We were so far gone, the knocking at the door was like background music trying to outdo the slapping of Kelanie's ass against my thighs. It wasn't until I heard the bass of Tatum's voice added to the symphony that slowed our flow.

"Karden, we're about to start the meeting."

The only response he got was more ass slapping and Kelanie's latest screams of her orgasmic release.

To be honest, the last thing I want to think about is the fact that my Chief and best friend got our Mistress pregnant because of *his* fear of her leaving. Now because of his insecure ass, *our* dreams have to die and she might have a seed in her that can probably control snakes better than she can. According to the traditional law, we have to produce male heirs for the future pack leader. Remembering that vow, I slide out of my mates' anus, got back on my knees and went back to pounding the pussy. She clenched tight, then released. She did this several times as my nut started to build. I stared down in her beautiful brown eyes knowing I will die the day she dies, if she does not survive that fucking birthing ritual.

My seed flowed hot and heavy in Kelanie's womb. Her face glowed like the start of a beautiful day. Except for the fact just an hour ago we were cleaning a snake infested palace.

With seamen and sweat covering our joined bodies, I looked down at my better half. Her eyes still glazed with desire. "Are you ready to get the day started?"

"After what I been through this morning? I can't think of a better way to start," she said smiling.

~~~

Dressed in nothing but white linen slacks and my hair hanging down my back, my mate dressed in a white silk mini dress, we were the last to arrive. The room was quiet, but the emotions spoke volumes. Jameria actually look like she could kill everyone in the damn room. This is bad. This is so bad. Damn, Tatum really fucked up.

Before we went on our last hunt, the Mistress told us we would be leaving the island for a few years, entering into college life. She had had a house set up inthe States for us. But thanks to our selfish ass, soon-to-be-Chief, we're stuck here until his heir reaches the proper age, or worse.......If Jameria and our mates don't make it through the "Birthing Ritual."

"Okay, from the look of things, it seems the snakes are attracted to the baby. Tatum told me the story my grandmother told him before leaving the States. If what she told him is true, then I will defiantly have to leave. The people of Geri do not need to be frighten of something I don't understand my-damn-self. We cannot let anyone find out about this pregnancy, yet," she said shaking her head.

"What story?" Tyce asked. She like the rest of the female mates was intrigued. Unlike Shyamae' and Carmen who actually knew and grew up with parents, the rest of the girls were pretty much on their own until Jameria found them.

Tatum went to the door and locked it before taking a seat in his black high back chair. He reached his hand out to Jameria and she went to him with no hesitation. Pulling her into his lap, she straddled him and placed her head on his shoulder. He circled his arms around her and grabbed her ass so he could position her just right over his groin. His body relaxed as she made the deep arch in her smooth bronze bare back, the white silk pants outlining the shape of her firm ass. This sensual position is known as 'Tatum's Stress Reliever.'

He was deep in thought. Deciding if he should repeat what was meant for his ears only. After the long debate within himself, he began.

"The story of Ella D's pregnancy is a gruesome tale that I will censor the best I can. I remember while my brothers and uncle was loading up in the truck and Jameria was busy retrieving the last of her things. Ms. Pat Ann, Jameria's grandmother came up to me and told me not to say anything, just listen. She said that during Jameria's mother pregnancy the house would stay covered in snakes. She said Ella D had gotten so scared, she was going to have an abortion. Hearing this, the snakes started hissing and striking out at her, until Ella D., kept repeating over and over that she was sorry for her ugly thoughts of taking the life of the innocent child. She said the snakes never trusted her alone with the unborn child. They would even lie in the bathroom while she bathe just to make sure the fetus is not harmed.

"Ms. Pat Ann delivered Jameria and she said the snakes never left the baby's side until the day her mother decided it was best that she left the child with her grandmother. Only then did the snakes dissipate and went their separate ways until the night a group of southern hospitality women decided to pay Ms. Pat Ann a visit and bring her some supplies that would be of help for the little one. Ms. Pat Ann's theory was that the snakes only appear when Jameria calls for them or.......when they feel she's being threaten."

The room was completely quiet, everyone deep in thought, coming to the same conclusion. Someone on the island hates Jameria so much, that the palace is turning into a new age snake pit.

Tatum stared at me, waiting for my reaction. I looked deep into his wise hazel eyes. Then they shifted over to Tyvine. No words had to be spoken. This went way beyond Tatum's insecurities, this was bigger than Motif, and it don't have shit on that damn "Birthing Ritual."

It was never about Jameria leaving him.

When we were fifteen, Tatum, Tyvine, and I were training with the wolves, when two black strays ran into our play, one male the other female. Both were friendly enough and eager for our attention, until one of our own wolves became jealous and tried to attack the stray male wolf. The female went after our wolf's throat. Before we could separate the three, eight more wolves came charging from the wild jungle. By this time we'd gotten the three apart, the male stray let out a loud bark, stopping his pack in their tracks. We stared in disbelief. Accompanying the two older strays were two young black males, one tan and one white bitch, and four pups (two tan and black and the other two black and white), their little paws just now bringing them to the party.

Unbelievable. Three generations in the same pack. The two young males walked up taking the flanks of their parents, the mates far back behind the older wolves, keeping their pups out of harm's way. The entire time Tatum was enchanted. He later told us his greatest goal. To create a army. And not just any army..........a family. At first I thought he was crazy, until Tyvine said that he can see it happening. They both smiled at each other with mischief in their eyes. Since I thought it was a stupid idea, one I didn't think he would take seriously, I said, "Yeah man, go for it."

My dumbass.

I looked up in time to see the faint smile that appeared on Tyvine's face. This was something that he wanted just as bad as Tatum. The wolf family intrigued the two so, I had no idea it had this big of effect on them.

"I'll have to leave or *"Geri Island"* will be a *"Deserted Island."* Jameria rose from Tatum's lap stretching, and then straighten the white silk triangles covering her plump breast.

"Why not get married now?" Of course Boaz wants the marriage to happen right away. Hell, Jameria has been like a surrogate mother since we met her. But something about the way she stared at Boaz made him drop his eyes to the floor, and then she turned her cold gaze on his mate. Shyamae' held her gaze for as long as she could until, like Boaz, her eyes strayed to the floor.

Jameria smiled her sweetest smile (the one Demarcus called her "killer smile") and said, "I find it very interesting Boaz, how you keep pushing for an early wedding. How about, you let me and Tatum worry about our relationship, while you and your mate do the same."

Boaz snapped his head back like he'd been slapped.

Knock. Knock. Knock.

Boaz, Pierce, and their mates went into Jameria's bedroom, taking the enchased vipers with them, before Tatum opened the door.

"Council would like to see you now." Motif's bodyguard had the audacity to smirk in his face.

The problem was Jameria saw it too. "The next time you disrespect my mate, your ass is going to be food for my snakes." Then, after a moment of thought. "Better yet, it might not be a next time." He immediately wiped the smirk off his face, leading us to the Council Hall.

We entered in our usual formation, leaving the Chief and Mistress dead center. Then we broke again, with our mates taking our flanks. Tatum and Jameria at the starter point of the V formation.

Motif was staring daggers at us.

When his eyes scan the group and landed on Tatum, he narrowed them into slits, showing how much he loathe his own son. And from the look on Tatum's face the feeling was mutual. A face so much like his mothers, with none of Motif's genes, not even one characteristic to tie them together. The one thing they do have in common is the pure hate they have for each other. And the air was thick with it.

Tatum's bare chest rose and fell with the deep breaths he was taking. His six foot, five inch muscular lean frame had tilted forward slightly. Jameria grabbed his arm knowing he would pounce on the man without thought. He relaxed his position and placed his arm around his mate's waist. Motif sneered at the act of affection. "Where are Pierce and Boaz? Where is my son! Why is he not here with the rest of your pack?!"

I wonder if Motif had lost his mind. It's one thing to look and not speak, but speaking to Tatum like that with Jameria just leaping distance from his ass, is just ludicrous. But at least he has witnesses..........hmm, that's probably his angle, to give the Council a reason to find fault against the Mistress.

"Elder Mara, could you please have a word with the soon-to-be former Chief, about how he addresses my fiancé. Since we will be wedded within the month, respect and loyalty must be given by all of his subjects, especially by those who have to step down from such high positions," she said smiling directly at Motif.

I'm glad I taught myself the blank expression because everyone on Council was in a state-of-shock.

"Within a month?" Nuieve was smiling from ear to ear. Mara once told me Nuieve was the reason Tatum got an early start in his training as Chief.

"Bu it's so soon........Within a month? Why haven't you said anything before?" Demarcus looked hurt beyond repair. He stared at his favorite adopted daughter with confusion and sadness. Marriage was the last thing he'd expected to come from her lips. He knew Jameria had goals she wanted to accomplish before she wedded. Hell, he wanted so much for Jameria that she really did live the princess life with a doting father.

He'd introduced her to the *"High Society"* life a few days after she was announced Mistress of Gerillian Island at the age of thirteen. Taking her on shopping sprees across the country, trips to Paris, Germany, China, Africa, Cuba and the list goes on. He adored his daughter, as if she was his flesh and blood. He'd adopted the rest later when they were between the ages of fifteen and sixteen and he loved all of them, but Jameria was the first of his adopted daughters. And because he's an elder who adopted all the girls, that guaranteed them a spot to stand as our mates, if we choose.

"I asked for her hand on my eighteenth birthday. We agreed to marry after Boaz and Pierce found their mates," Tatum said with honest sincerity. He, like the rest of us knew how much this had to be hurting Demarcus.

I felt the shit coming, but I just didn't know how to stop it from hitting the fan. I'm hoping this little episode was rehearsed amongst our Mistress and Chief, because just yesterday she was trying to kill him for knocking her up.

"You're giving Boaz a month to find his mate? He's too young and Noonie and I will start grooming him to marry the daughter of the Meeba tribe. I will *not* allow him to mate with a female-freak-of-nature," Motif all but growled.

Tyvine and Tatum were making very subtle movements toward each other with Jameria in the middle. To the naked eye, our formation never changed, but our pack saw the easy rearranging and moved ever so slightly to accommodate with the ruse.

"You forget that I started my training years ahead of my time. And understand this; Boaz is a part of my pack, not yours............Besides, he's already found a mate."

Motif snapped.

Chapter 2

Tyvine…………………..

It took everything I had to hold Cougar *and* Jameria back, plus not jump in my-damn-self, as Tatum and Motif had it out.

Motif jumped off the podium and headed straight for Tatum. At the same time, I grabbed Jameria around her waist, (who was already leaning into her defensive crouch) and slammed my hand over Cougar's mouth, to halt her cat call.

Tatum met him halfway and close hung his ass. This was an ass whipping waiting to happen.

Motif's retired pack stood to the side and watched him lose his title right before their very eyes. Since this fight was taking place in the Council Hall, the last man standing is the ruler. If Motif had stepped down, he would have had a spot on the Council as an Elder, but by him challenging his son, he can kiss that title good bye too. Motif saw his reign sinking down the drain when Jameria shocked the crowd with the wedding announcement. And Tatum flushed it by saying Boaz found his mate. Which reminds me, when would be a good time to tell Tatum that Boaz is already fucking?

When I burst into Shyamae's room to tell her to stay put until they cleared the snakes, I caught his ass knee deep in pussy. And the way he was working her, couldn't have been their first time.

Jameria calmed down when Tatum drew blood. He'd beaten Motif's head against the pearl white marble floor, for what felt like hours, but only minutes passed. When he lost consciousness, Council demanded Tatum to stop. But only one person can control this Chief and she also controls this island. The people of Geri Island adore Jameria. If she doesn't live through the birthing process, there just might be a riot.

She tapped my hand that was still secure around her abdomen, and then took her time, making her way to Tatum.

"Tyvine, let me go. I can clear this whole room with just one cat," Cougar whispered. As I glanced around me, I noticed the rest of my brothers were doing their best to hold their own mates back. Watching their young Chief being attacked was a surprise they didn't count on.

"No. Motif challenged Tatum. Chief against Chief. No pack member from either side can interfere." And even if we could, I wouldn't let my mate anywhere near the retired pack.

It was rumored that a gang rape was planned for one of our pack mates. Though, it might be Jameria they're after, but even I know one won't be enough for the ole bastards. Motif lead his pack down a worthless path with no real glory days and

nothing to look forward to. They were deemed to stay on this island with no real aspect of the world. Bragging rights and their so called honor is at stake. Being called old and useless in their thirties and forties with so much of their life ahead of them, has finally taken its toll.

Instead of Motif stepping down gracefully and taking a position as an elder when his time came, he decides to fight his eldest son who's groomed to run this island anyway…………….. Something's not adding up. Like why would Jameria make the younger pack members stay in her bedroom…………….and the strange looks she kept giving Boaz and Shyamae.'

Something is defiantly going on.

Jameria grabbed Tatum's fist in mid-air, pressing it against her stomach. He immediately calmed and stood, easing his bloody hand into hers.

Motif's pack removed his body to join Noonie's in the physical rehab ward.

"Well, this has been an interesting meeting Chief Tatum," Elder Nuieve said with pride and admiration oozing from his pores. He wore the same awe struck expression he had since our first council meeting as a pack. "When can we meet young Boaz's mate?"

Tatum looked into Elder Marlease, Pierce's father eyes as he spoke. "Pierce has a mate also."

By him being one of the young elders like Demarcus, Marlease usually don't voice his opinion. But this time his face held a huge smile. "I'm quite sure he's as happy as the rest of you seem to be with your young mates. Please send them to me. Let me meet the newest member of our family."

By this time, happy tears were streaming down his face. Jameria once told us that he and Pierce are very close. Tatum had actually remembered Marlease and his wife were close also.....until she gave birth. The last day of her life. Tatum said the only reason he remembered was because his mother cried for days. She was his mother's best friend.

Smiling, Tatum said, "How about I send them back. My pack and I have many things to discuss."

"Of course," Nuieve said as he clapped his hands together coming back to the podium with the biggest smile on his face I'd ever seen. "So is the wedding still a month from today?"

"Yes, but......," Jameria said looking innocently sad.

"What is it Jameria? You know you can tell us anything," Nuieve said with pure sincerity, falling face first into her web. The Council always gave her whatever shewanted. Demarcus gave her a huge allowance, clothes, and jewelry. And the rest of the elders gave her houses, cars, boats, islands, even a fucking diamond mine! So this was no surprise. They have always been putty in her hands.

"Well, July 15th is a special day for me. It's the day my grandmother died. I would love to get married on the day I feel closest to her."

"That's two weeks from now. You want to plan a wedding in ten days?"

Like the pro I know her best for, she batted her lashes, placed both hands in Tatum's, putting her soft swollen breast against his shoulder, and ducked her head shyly saying, "Actually I already have it planned. I really don't want to rush you if it will be a problem."

"No. No, Jameria, if there is anything you need help with, please be sure to let us know. July 15th is your wedding day to the new Chief of Gerillian Island. As far as Noonie goes, (which is why we called this meeting in the first place), I understand she came into your room unannounced and tried to seduce you," Nuieve said. "Would you like to have her band?"

"No, she's Motif's mate. It is up to him what to do with her, just as long as she leaves me and my pack alone."

"I totally understand young Chief. We do not want to keep you and your pack from your obligations. Let us know what you want us to do and we will wait here for young Boaz and Pierce to introduce their mates."

"Thank you," Tatum said, already heading toward the doors.

We walked out in a straight line with our mates close to our sides. Cougar was more fidgety than before the fight started. The cause is being overdue for her tongue bath, thanks to those damn snakes.

When we entered Jameria's suite, we found Boaz lounging on the couch with the vipers wrapped around his arms, asleep. Pierce, Shyamae' and Carmen stood to the side staring.

"How long have he been like this?"

"Since you left for the meeting," Shyamae' said eyeing Jameria. The Mistress held the young girls' stare, as if waiting on her to make a move. "It was like he was in a trance or something. He just went into the Mistress room and held his arms in the cage without a thought."

Jameria just hunched her shoulders. "Well I doubt if the snakes was calling him to pick them up. Anyway, you know how Boaz is. When it comes to animals and him, nothing surprises me." She turned from the girl and face Pierce and his mate with a smile. "Go prepare yourselves. The Council wants to meet the newest mates."

Shyamae' stood mesmerized by what the Mistress said, like a dream come true, while Tatum removed the snakes (who went to him easily) from Boaz.

Boaz woke looking around himself confused. "How did the meeting go?"

"Your brother is now Chief of Geri Island. Him and Jameria is due to marry in two weeks," Moham said grinning.

First his reaction was shocked, then confused, before he looked to his mate. Then he jumped up and threw both arms around Jameria. "Are you serious..........two weeks........the council actually went for that?"

"Let's just say the Mistress left them no mercy. You have to go prepare for council. They are ready to meet your new mates." I could actually see happiness in Tatum's eyes before him and Jameria shared a strange look.

He'd been miserable since the meeting he had with me, Karden, Cole, and Moham yesterday. He called a meeting with just us guys, reminding us about one of the laws in the tradition book. By us being in his pack, we must procreate to produce heirs to follow in the Chief's heir pack.

"What about Motif," Boaz asked.

"He won't be there........Go get dressed. They're waiting for you."

Tatum then turn his attention to Karden after they left, knowing he'll be the first with questions. Over the years the Chief has become more lenient with us. Letting us get away with little things like this. But to be honest, Karden just gets on my fucking nerves with that shit.

"You're marrying in two weeks. Are you sure about this?"

I knew Karden didn't want this wedding to take place,

since Jameria told us about her plans for us in the States. Hell, I wanted it too.............but not as much as to what Tatum had in mind. I saw how the wheels were turning in that brain of his as soon as that family pack of wolves showed up. But it was the pups that were fascinating. Creating a life that can control several sets of animals at one time..........

"I know it's soon but I've already started gaining weight, and I don't know when this fetus will have us smothered beneath a bed of snakes or worse, if it can control anything else."

"Do you mean the wolves?" Kelanie's eyes were the size of silver dollars.

"I don't know yet, but I'm just in my second month. Imagine what will happen in another month as my pregnancy progress."

Everyone was speechless and Tatum was looking as guilty as ever.

Jameria stood in front of him, pulling his face to hers, blocking his emotions from our view. "You're all dismissed. We will meet for lunch to discuss the wedding."

I lead Cougar's fidgety ass to her suite and locked the door. Hers was at the very end of the north wing hall, which was a good thing.

Cougar already had my pants down around my ankles, licking me like she was starving. I removed the rest of my clothes preparing myself for her daily tongue bath. Like a mother cat cleaning its kitten, my body was hers for the taking.

On her knees sucking my twelve point two inch pole, she backed me up to her leopard print couch, pushing me down. Her tongue and hands were everywhere; my inner thighs, my chest, my neck, back, having me to turn over as she made her way to my ass. Her tongue caressed and penetrated my anus, while messaging my balls. My dick was so hard I felt precum glide down my shaft. It must've caught her attention, because her strong smooth fingers were pulling the head back, running her tongue along my shaft like the best flavor in the world is my dick.

I rose a little higher on my knees allowing her full access. Her nose was buried deep in my balls, trying to get as much of me in her mouth as she could.

As soon as the first orgasm hit me, Cougar proceeded to strap herself in the swing in her playroom. I had her sitting area converted into a playroom equipped with every sexual toy I could think of or imagine. My Cougar was insatiable. Thick and wild, curly red hair, and smooth skin the color of the lightest cappuccino, and firm large breast I just love smothering my face in every day. Her 5'9 frame was the best weapon any man could ask for. She could kill you with her bare hands and make your wildest dreams come true, all at the same time.

I strapped her lower part high in the air with one leg going east and the other going west. Kissing the little paw print tattoos on her hairless mound, I lubed my arm from wrist to elbow. Her honey and coconut scent surrounded me as I pulled her pearl between my lips, and then began to stroke her anus. She purred when I started to penetrate her slowly. Pulling my face deeper between her legs, her grind on my hand increased. Each finger added had her moaning from pure bliss that made my dick get hard all over again. By the time my fist entered her anus, her sweet juices coated my face and lined my stomach. She suctioned my arm deeper in her ass as my own semen coated the silk black sheets.

'Release me Tyvine."

Her shaky voice caused me to look up into eyes so glazed with desire, my heart faltered. I removed my arm and released her bindings, allowing her to push me on my back. She climbed on top with her ass facing me, milking my dick with each roll of her hips. The feeling was so intense, I had trouble controlling my shaking hand as it reentered her anus.

She leaned forward telling me to "go deeper" causing even more friction to my dick through her ass. I grabbed her wild curly mane with my other hand, pulling her pussy down hard on me.

I came instantly.

While her orgasm hit her from every direction, she laid flat on her chest with her ass in the air. I worked my arm in and out of her anus while she sucked the remainder of my nectar from my balls. Her body was shaking so uncontrollably, her ass shook straight to sleep. As I pulled her close to me and covered our bodies, I thought about her first night on the island. My brothers and sisters (what we refer to our pack from time to time) thought our first time was in the wolves cage. Actually, it was her first night here.

After the party Noonie had for us on the beach, I asked Cougar to show me her cat den. The hike was only thirty minutes from the palace, which was still too damn close to civilians. At first I thought her fidgety walk was natural, but of course I was wrong. In the den her lioness was in the middle of tongue bathing. I heard a little moan beside me and looked to see Cougar licking her lips. She'd go from fidgeting to shaking.

"Are you alright?" I thought she was about to have a seizure.

"I'm fine. After commotions or confrontations, I tend to feel anxious and dirty. So like my felines here, only a bath will suffice."

That didn't seem like such a big problem, so I grabbed her hand so we could head back to the palace. Instead she snatched away and sat on the ground against the cool cave wall.

"What's wrong now," I asked a little confused.

She didn't answer.

Instead she started to lick from her wrist to her fingertips.

She spread her legs so that her knees touched the cave walls. Then in amazing flexibility she bent the top half of her torso forward until she tasted her own pussy.

The scent of her was so intoxicating and the exotic position she presented to me, left no questions of doubt at the moment.

Not caring if her cats attacked me, I made my way on my knees, between her thighs, diving into the divine feast. Her coconut scent was more concentrated between her silky thighs and the first taste was all I needed to lose control. Soon I became territorial, hearing myself growl with madness as I devoured her juices.

After her fifth orgasm her body was totally relaxed, but her glazed green eyes was asking for more. That's when I realized my mate had an uncanny fetish.

Right there, in the cold dense cave, Cougar took my hand and shoved the whole thing in her anus. Still in the state-of-shock, she pushed me flat on my back and rode my arm like she was on a pogo stick. By this time, my dick was rock hard and the blue silk pants did nothing to hide my excitement.

Not that it needed to be hidden from her.

She rose off my arm slowly, and then penetrated her tight pussy on my dick. As I felt her hymn break, I was amazed this was her first time.

Later that evening when I asked her about it, she explained her cats was all she knew. 'So learning from them, I pleased myself by cleansing myself.'

Cougar said when Jameria found her, she was surrounded by a den full of cats and her father (which was a fucking lion, king of the fucking jungle) stood at the lead. She said that he was ready to attack but a snake the size of the tallest tree in the rain forest, dove in front of her ready to swallow her leader hold. 'But the beautiful black girl stopped the snake with just the lift of her hand when she saw me jump forward to save my father.' She said she had never seen anyone like her.

Poachers always roam the forest of Madagascar so that was nothing new. That's how she kept up with the different languages she spoke. She'd spy on them from a distance and created a technique for her to learn what the hunters were doing or planning to do. It made it easier for her to protect the animals she loved. But Jameria was no hunter, at least not the kind

Cougar's use to. She said the beautiful girl spoke to her in several languages until she stop on one she understood. Telling her that she'd come here to find a mate for her brother. She told her she could offer a safe life for her and her cats if she was willing to learn a little etiquette and stand by him, for he will be one of the future leaders of an Island. Cougar said she was intrigued by the beautiful girl, and then the rest of the girls after Jameria cloaked her and brought her back to Demarcus. She said she'd never laid

her eyes upon a man who was so beautiful, almost God like.

Other than hunters, Cougar never had the "pleasure" (her word, not mine) to meet a man who actually turns her on so much that "white stuff" (her words, not mine) started to run down her thighs. She told me that the black girl saw where all her attention was at, smiled and told her to be patient, that she would have one of her own when they made it here to the Island. And she was buoyed, because Jameria did not disappoint. Cougar told me the first time she laid eyes on me, she knew that I belonged to her. "'But Jameria said that you had to choose me. I thought I was going to go crazy when I saw you going to one of the other girls. Then for no reason you just turned around and stared at me.'"

Which was true. I had no idea who Jameria had picked for me. All of the girls at Noonie's party were all similar in some kind of way. Expensive jewelry, lots of make-up, and stuck-the-fuck-up. When I was about to give-up and just talk to one of the locals, the wild red head caught my attention. And when she looked at me with those hypnotic green eyes, I was a goner. I didn't care whose guest she was. At the end of that day, she was going to be mine. And taking the words from my beautiful mate, 'Jameria did not disappoint.' There's not another woman in this world that can get me excited like Cougar. And if there is, I don't want to meet her.

Like the rest of the mates, Cougar is an orphan who was adopted by Demarcus. But Cougar lead the most salvaged life of them all. Her childhood was nothing like any of the other mates.

Cougar was lost in the woods when she was two years old. Her biological father was a researcher who went on an expedition with his wife and daughter from Canada who was never heard from again. From what Jameria was able to gather, Cougar's father was a famous biologist, studying plant life in the rainforest. She later found reports where the 'Expedition for New Plant Life" ended and a "Search and Rescue" began. The rescue mission was eventually called off when traces of the young couple's remnants was found bloody and rip to shreds.

Once Jameria told me the whole story, I didn't know how to take something like that. I had started to have doubts about the sexy feline female, the Mistress picked for me. The poor girl wasn't even raised the common way. Hell, it was years down the line before she found out what a shack was. Especially after hearing her father who raised her was a feline actually walking on four legs. Out of the entire bunch, Cougar was the wildest.

Not pampered.

Not sheltered.

Straight salvage.

A woman willing to die for me without question and boarder line crazy.

To prove a point, this crazy bitch made one of Motif's guards torture himself to death, for two-fucking-days straight.

The shit was sick……….which was why I wanted her. My mind was made up.

Not because she made the man chew broken glass and digest it. The reason *why* she made him do it was because disrespecting me in front of Cougar caused him his life.

Shit like that turns me the-fuck-on.

As part of our traditional rule, young pack members have to train to one day take our proper positions as personal guards to the Chief. Once the pack reaches the ages sixteen they can request a challenge through the Council to go to battle against the lead Guards. The new Pack gets up to three tries before they're deemed not worthy to stand as 'Ruling Pack.'

Our Pack won the very first battle, leaving a few broken and unrecognizable. Boaz and Pierce were too young at the time but their help was not necessary. The five of us stood before Council drenched in blood, with big smiles on our faces. Our chests heaving, adrenaline still pumping in our veins. Yet, some of those from Motif's Pack managed to walk away talking shit. One of the guards actually made the comment that he'd rather eat glass than pass his lead rank over to me.

And Cougar made him do just that.

Later that night, after the palace was sound asleep, Cougar's Black Panther, Sasha entered the guard's quarters so quietly, that it took the man twenty minutes before he woke-up and realized she was over him. The poor man pissed *and* shitted his pants.

The room reeked!

That didn't matter to Cougar, she pulled Sasha back off the bed and told the man to get his ass up. "'You got a promise to keep bitch.'"

She'd pulled one of the chairs from the dining room table and had me to take a seat at one end of the table and the guard at the other while she went tohis refrigerator to retrieve a beer for me and a wine cooler for herself. As I chatted with her in idle conversation she was in the kitchen with several pieces of the man's finest china in the blinder. She then poured the finely crushed pieces in a crystal bowl and told the man to eat up. It wasn't like he had a choice. Sasha was lounging right there at his feet in front of a box fan Cougar had found to blow the man's fowl scent in another direction.

As he dined, Cougar told him a little story about a man who disrespected her heart. She told him that she never saw many men growing up and the first one she talked to was so good to her that she called him her heart. She said the only thing she have in this world is her heart and her cats, and she would do anything to protect both. She looked him in his eyes as he died and said, "'Tyvine is my heart. Since you can't abide by his rules, I see no reason why you shouldn't get everything you ask for.'"

My gift to her was giving his body to one of Jameria's snakes as our little secret.

Chapter 3

Moham…………

I stood in my defensive crouch with my arms wide and my knees bent, feet spread far apart. Tyce seated on my back with her feet on each of my thighs, positioning herself with one hand on my shoulder and whip dangling in the air from her other hand.

Three feet in front of me, Tatum and his mate mirrored our exact pose. They're position looking more feline. Jameria pounced first, sending her whip out and around Tyce's arm, pulling her to the ground, as she took her place on my back. Positioning her leg perfectly around my neck, her right leg manage to make it all the way around with the back of her thigh pressing hard against my jugular. She twisted her left leg behind my back locking her right one as she brought me to my knees with her signature choke hold. Jameria then flipped backwards on her hands demonstrating how easy it would be to snap my neck.

But instead, she released me grinning from ear to ear.

"Maybe next time Mo."

"You know, Mistress pregnant women normally take long walks on the beach or sit on the deck with a good book. Fighting in the jungle with two men and a bear leading woman, does not consist of relaxing," I said trying to catch my breath.

Jameria was always happy during training. I like to call this her free time.

"I guess I'm just one of those women who have to stay active."Poor Mistress. She misunderstood the concept between an active woman and an active *pregnant* woman.

"I don't think that kind of active is healthy."

I expected the negative reaction from Jameria, but my sweet Tyce looked about ready to slap the taste out of my mouth. Since I told her that I had to knock her up, training has been hell on me. Her punches have been a little harder and twice she'd slipped slicing her blade into me during our knife dance, saying it was an accident.

Accident my ass.

Tyce never misses during a knife fight.

"Do you expect me to stop training during my entire pregnancy Moham? I admit that I'll have to slow down and be careful, but does that mean I have to stop being who I am?"

I looked to Tatum for help. He'd leaned against a tree drying sweat from around his neck, with a stupid ass grin on his face. It was obvious I wasn't going to get any help from him.

Jameria and Tyce both dressed in jeans and bikini tops (looking sexy enough to take the world) stared at me with their fists propped on their curvy hips, waiting for my response.

"I meant no harm ladies. Please let me offer my most sincere apology. You see, the women who are born and raised on this island are normally pampered from the moment they find out they're pregnant all the way up to the child's first birthday. I wasn't implying in any way that you were-"

"Don't worry about it Mo. I was raised by a *traiteur* the first decade of my life. She didn't leave this world without teaching me a few things……..which reminds me, we have a lot to do before the wedding. Tyce don't forget to get all of the girls dress sizes before we leave for the mainland tomorrow," Jameria said as Tatum grabbed her around her waist and lead her back to the palace.

I turned my attention back to my mate. Her white albino skin had tanned to a natural cream, enhancing the delicate pinkshade in her cheeks. A woman who never thought twice about her looks, yet her natural beauty still takes my breath away, even to this day.

She retrieved our towels, tossing mine to me as she made her way to the palace. I followed, dreading the journey I was about to take.

Tyce is ovulating.

So now I have to drag my ass in here and make a baby. Tatum is so far up my shit list now, that it's going to take the end of the world to get him off. This just might be the first time in my life that I *won't* be enjoying the sex. Lately, I don't think any of the guys really been happy, except for Boaz and Pierce. When I entered the north wing, Tyce had already unlocked her sitting room door. She went into her closets so I decided to run a bath. Maybe if she relaxed for a while, then I'll relax.

She came in behind me as I got undressed. When I faced her, I slipped my arms around her small waist and my tongue into her mouth. Kissing Tyce was like eating a peach for hours. Which is what we did her first night with me.

I was already excited when we went to the beach after our first hunt. The Mistress had found me a gifted female of my very own. The problem was that I didn't know who she was or what she looked like. But her scent was another story of its' own.

The scent of peaches invaded my senses like a hurricane. Soon my nose lead me to the pale face and gray eyes of Tyce. She was standing in a snug off the shoulder silk mini dress, sucking on fresh peeled peach slices. Those silver dollar gray eyes was so focused on my face that the little dark curly hair girl she was talking to, had to snap her fingers twice before catching her attention again to let her know she was leaving with Cole.

As soon as Cole and his little Maria left, I approached her introducing myself as her future. She laughed at me. At first I was furious that she didn't take me serious, but soon I was listening to her singing laugh. It was so melodious that I began laughing myself......then leaning toward her lips, until mine touched hers. To this day, I still don't know how we manage to wrap our arms around each other in the middle of a crowded party. Her juicy pink lips were so sweet, her mouth was my hors d'oeuvre for the rest of the night.

I was shocked when the Mistress gave me the brief description of Tyce. A girl from the Algonquian tribe in Canada who left her band on her own. Jameria went on to say that Tyce had a wonderful childhood and many friends. Her parents loved her dearly and would have died a thousand deaths just to see her again. When I finally got to know my mate better I asked her why she would leave such a happy band of people.

"To keep them safe," she'd said. "I was thirteen when my gifts were fully developed.....and also uncontrollable. The bears refused to keep their distance and I didn't want my family to know and be frightened. One day my father found me in the woods cuddled-up sleep against a grizzly and nearly had a heart attack. Later that night he came to my room and apologized for over reacting. He told me that my blood is of the original Algonquian people before the big cultural change. He told me that in this day and time it meant that I was special, and he would love me always. But even though my parents loved me continuously, I felt the change each time I walked into a room or tried to sit down at the dinner table with them. Fear. They were afraid of me or of what I had become. So I went to the wilderness to live among the bears. I learned a lot in those three years about my gift than I did the first thirteen years of my life."

She smiled with a faraway look on her pretty face staring out into the late Brazilian sun. "The day Jameria came for me, I was in the middle of helping a grizzly give birth. The sow's labored breath was cut short in the cold cave when she walked in. Her bronzed skin wrapped in white fur looked like a chocolatediamond sitting on a bed of clouds. Beautiful. In all of her white, she got on manicured hands and wool pantsuit knees and asked, "'What do you need me to do to help?'" That day I gain my very first real friend who took my weakness and made it my strength. For that alone I'll always be grateful." Then she looked at me with that smile I love oh-so-much and said, "The rest was a bonus."

Now we're both in the bathtub about to make love for the first time without a condom. While the rest of the girls in the pack took birth control pills, I asked Tyce not to. I wanted her body to stay as natural as possible.

She snuggled her head against my chest, rotating her plump ass against my erection, causing me to focus all of my attention on her and the rhythm of her hips. I grabbed the loofah sponge and used some of her peach and mango body wash to saturate it before running it between her 38D mounds. Using my other hand, I angled her head so I could taste her lushes pink lips again. My arousal had hit such a high point, that it began slapping the middle of her back. Breaking the kiss, she stood and wrapped a big yellow towel around her body and made her way to the bedroom without drying off.

I immediately unstopped the tub and followed her into the bedroom where Jazmine Sullivan was begging for her man back. Tyce laid across the bed with her legs up and waiting. Tonight there will be no foreplay.

This is something that I was not ready for and the part I skipped in the old book. *My* focus was on the adventure, learning new things, going on epic journeys around the world, and fighting for something that seems magical and right at the same time.

No. Tonight it's going to be straight fucking......at least I thought.

I had no idea that as soon as I entered her sticky sweet walls for the first time without a shield my animal side would kick in this swiftly. I was so taken by it, I flipped her over, bit into her flank and rode her ass until her entire body was beet red. And yet, I've spilled my seed in her numerous times tonight, the wolf in me refuses to be taunted by words of rest and sleep.

3:00 a.m.

Outside the bedroom window, the clouds parted, letting the full moon be my guide to the fragrance that called to me in my dreams. Though I was fully awake, it seems the dream was still in motion. The real part is, I'm about to mount my mate. The dream part, even though my brothers are not in this very room with me, I feel them. I can feel exactly what they feel at this very moment. But unfortunately for our mates, it's not going to be anything good.

"Mo, what's wrong?"

I looked up to see Tyce concern eyes staring back at me. I couldn't say anything. I could only feel. Lucky for her, this is not the first time this has happened. But it *was* too late to run.

As soon as it registered to her what was about to happen, she tried to bolt. I caught her by her hair and slammed her ass back down on the bed straddling her. When I looked up, her small fist caught me right in the eye. But I didn't let that stop me. My dick was so hard, my head started to ache from the pain.

I grabbed Tyce arms and held them over her head as I leaned forward and bit into her jugular with just the slightest pressure. She immediately stop fighting and spread her legs instead.

I didn't wait.

I plunged deep into her, flexing my thirteen inch rod as her walls adjusted to my size. I fucked her unmercifully as did my brothers to their mates. I rose up and stared at the moon as I pounded the love of my life into the custom made mattress. But I just couldn't stop.

Then I felt it.

It hit me so hard, I hadn't notice that I was standing in the bed, while Tyce was doing her best to climb the wall to get away from me. I caught her by her hair again and pulled her ass down hard on my swollen dick, forcing her to accept this nut. I raised her up and pulled her down hard again, grinding myself so hard against her pelvic bone, I tried to push my whole fucking body inside her wet, raw pussy. The third and last time, I pulled her down on me, caused howls that vibrated through the north wing. I felt each and every one of my brothers release at the same time I felt mine.

Un-fucking-believable.

The next morning, I woke-up in bed alone. That wasn't surprising. All of the girls went to the mainland to be fitted for their dresses. I got up to get my day started when I heard voices in the sitting room.

Tatum, Karden, Tyvine, and Cole was in the small kitchenette, talking over cups of coffee and beignets.

"What's up," I said grabbing my mate's favorite mug.

"Tyce told us you were still in bed, so we decided to have breakfast in here." Tyvine being the only one of us who likes nutmeg in his coffee was searching through the cabinets. "We need to talk about what happened last night."

So, it wasn't a dream.

"When I woke-up this morning, Maria was standing over me with a blade at my throat," Cole said biting into his beignet. "If Jameria and Tatum hadn't come in when they did, I'd probably be dead."

This shit is getting out of hand. "What are we going to do? The next tournament is three years away and I don't think any of us will last that long."

Tatum, the only one of us who didn't seem concern about the fact that our mates might kill us during the next full moon said, "Don't worry. I got a plan."

Damn.

The last time he said he had a plan, our Mistress ended up pregnant.

He saw the skepticism in our faces. "Look, I know all of you are still pissed at me for all the bullshit I'm putting you through, but please just hear me out."

"Okay," Karden said after a long sigh. "Let's hear it."

"Jameria asked the girls a while back about how they obtained their gifts. Other than Cougar and Jameria, the rest received theirs in a dream form. Since tonight is the last night of the full moon, I think we should spend the night in the jungle."

"But we've stayed in the jungle plenty of nights during a full moon. What makes this time so different," Karden asked.

It was Cole who answered him this time. "Enough of us just reached the proper age. You know that book Jameria obtained a while back, there's a passage in it that talks about when enough members in a wolf pack reaches adulthood, during a full moon."

"Yeah, but that was for an actual wolf pack Cole. We're human."

"Before the women left for the mainland, the ladies suggested that the five of us have a private bachelor party in the woods. Jameria agreed one night under a full moon without them on the island would be a good idea," Tatum said, knowing we'll go along with whatever the Mistress agrees to.

What a fucking disappointment. "So, I guess there will be no strippers."

"You guessed right," Tatum said standing. "We have a lot to prepare for, before the wedding tomorrow. I'll meet you guys at the edge of the woods tonight."

Cole stayed behind as everyone else filed out of the room. "What's on your mind, man? And don't start off with the lies. I have a lot to do today, so let's spare each other the argument."

"Fine. I attacked Tyce last night. She left this morning before I had the chance to talk to her."

"Well I saw her this morning and I am not going to lie to you dude. She looked pissed. But I don't think she'll leave you hanging."

"I know. I just don't know what came over me. One minute, I was holding her in my arms, then the next, I was choking the life out of her, while shoving my dick in her to the hilt.........I'm afraid what might happen next time," I said, biting into my beignet.

"At least you can remember what you did. The only thing I know is, the bedroom was fucked up and Maria was cursing me to a suffering life in hell.

"You really missed out this morning. Jameria and Tatum saved my ass, just as one of Maria's gorilla's bust the bedroom door down. When I realized what was going on, I hopped over Tatum's body after being tossed up against the wall like a rag doll. I ran my naked ass down the hall to Cougar's rooms for safety, hoping she would call one of her cats to kill this crazy bitch. Tyvine answered the door butt naked asking me why I didn't use my damn key, while monkeys and apes chased me down the hall and Maria putting roots on my ass in Spanish. So stop your damn whining, because what happened between you two was cheesecake compared to the morning I had," he said breaking off in laughter.

I was in tears. It took us both a while to get control over our laughing pains.

"I guess after you put it like that, whining about my little situation do seems insensitive right now."

We were both quiet for a moment. Then I asked what was really bothering me. "What do you think will happen tonight?"

"I don't know. But hopefully it's the answer to our problems."

Chapter 4

Cole..................

The stars normally makes an appearance, but the warm wind and cloud coverage is making that somewhat impossible. There was no need for a log fire on this night. Instead, the five of us slept on top of our sleeping bags. Pierce and Boaz slept in the north wing alone, while their mates tagged along with the rest of the girls to the mainland.

After Tatum took control of the palace, he ordered our entire pack to reside in the north wing. He wanted us as far away from Noonie and Motif as we could possibly get. The Elders wanted him to move into the royal chambers, but he told them he'd already taken the crown, "It'll be cruel to take his shelter too." He just didn't won't to sleep between the same four walls Motif and Noonie shared.

If we were being totally honest with ourselves, we were gradually distancing ourselves from the royal court for some time now. Since the girls moved here, we've barely slept in our own chambers in the main hall. But we knew Tatum did it to keep the young ones (Pierce and Boaz) closer to us since they are still under age.

"What do you think the girls are doing," Karden asked flipping flat on his back. "I don't know, but it has got to be more fun than this." Moham and

Karden was still a little pissed at Tatum for the shit we're in.

It's true that we are going a little bit too far, what we're about to do tomorrow, but I feel that Tatum was right in the choice he made. None of us planned to start our futures off like this, but the choice was never ours to begin with. The day Tatum chose us to be in his pack was the last day of our free lives. Yet, the life we live is *nothing* like I thought it would be. The day we found Jameria was actually the beginning of our lives. My brothers sees her as a living "Luandinha." A water goddess of the snakes. So taken in by her beauty that your focus is so lost, it's already too late, because she'd struck you dead.

Jameria is more of a sister, than a Mistress to me. For her I would die a thousand deaths, as if she was of my blood. Other times, I just want to beat the shit out of her for some of the things she do. There have been plenty of times at our dinner table with just us and our father arguing over something stupid. Demarcus Flask loved all of his adopted daughters ....but it's different with Jameria.

The first time I noticed our sibling closeness was during a fight we'd gotten into on a fishing trip we was on with our father. We was fifteen at the time. I had about an ounce of bud with me, but got the shit wet when the boat flipped over earlier that morning. I knew Jameria kept some in her vanity case. So when I went in it (without her permission), it was with her journal.......that I just so happen to be looking through when she caught me in her tent.

"'What the fuck are you doing,'" came the voice of the girl- I mean *woman*.....maybe freak is a better word to describe the shit Tatum and Jameria do in this book.

"'I came to get some bud,'" I said still reading.

"'Then get it and get out,'" she said, trying to snatch the book out of my hand.

I held it away from her smiling mockingly as she grabbed at her precious journal.

"'I wonder what dad would say if he knew his angel was on her knees swallowing his nephew's dick, while he's stuffing cherries in her ass? Do you think he'll still kiss those pretty little hands of yours, knowing you shoved each one in Tatum's ass as he fucked you up in yours? Let's go find out,'" I said moving around her, trying to get out of the tent.

She grabbed me around my neck and started banging my head against the packed ground. I slapped her across her face with the book, giving me enough time to scramble to one knee.

She grabbed the book out of my hand and the night lantern offthe floor.

That crazy bitch poured the oil from her night lantern on me and would have sat me on fire if I hadn't tackled her ass. I straddled her, then picked up the little bottle of cognac she snuck on the trip and toss that shit in her face. Demarcus heard the commotion and dragged both of us out the tent by our hair and went "Incredible Hulk" on our asses. Literally, my dad went 'ole school.' He'd lifted Jameria by her hair and used his left foot, kicking her in the chest, causing her body to slam hard against an old maple tree. He lifted me with his right hand and the uppercut he delivered dazed me long enough to grasp the understanding that this ass whipping won't end until I fight back.

He was on top of me delivering blow after blow. I couldn't get in a good shot nowhere. Jameria finally got him in a headlock, pulling him off of me. He flipped her on her back, about to go at her again, but not before I was on my feet to surprise him with a right hook, sending him to the ground.

Jameria recovered, removed her white t-shirt then flipped high in the air and positioned herself on my back in a move that has been practiced by her and Tatum so many times during training. A move they call, "The Attack Mode." Though, I'm not as good as Tatum, I could still hold my own.

I positioned my body in the three point stand as Jameria placed her feet on the top of my thighs, and leaned forward until the back of my head was nestled between her breasts. Across from us, Demarcus got into a stance of his own, with a curved blade in his hand.

I didn't have a sickle.

I had something better.

Jameria's body was my weapon.

Her bra and hair, my handle.

Reaching behind me and placing my hand between her firm mounds, I grabbed hold of the custom made bra with titanium wiring and flipped her over my head, launching her with feet pointed directly at Demarcus. He jumped high and landed a swift kick to her abdomen, sending her crashing to the ground.

I didn't wait.

I went at him with everything I had. Soon Jameria was back on her feet, fighting in a trio dance that could only guarantee death. Demarcus landed a triple kick combo, putting Jameria and me both on our asses.

I gave up.

Being younger does not guarantee victory all of the time. Lying flat on my back, I turned my head to the side and saw my sister mirroring my image. She was on her back panting for air. There was no more fight left in her.

Demarcus stood between us laughing like that was the most fun he'd had in his entire life. Then he calmed and said, "Boy, what the hell is wrong with you hitting a girl!? Didn't I raise you better than that? And Jameria, I don't give a damn if he post nude pictures of you on the internet, if you ever try to kill your brother again, I 'ma stomp your ass so far in the ground, it'll take a mole to find you."

That was the last time we fought like that, except during training. That's when we let our frustrations loose.

"Hey Cole, do you think Maria's going to show up tomorrow," Tyvine asked, with that stupid smirk on his face.

"Shut up."

They all burst out laughing.

"Whatever."

The shit really just not funny. If Maria don't come back, I might take out everyone on this damn island. I can't lose her. Not my better half. As soon as I saw her, I knew I had to have her. I didn't give a fuck if she was with Jameria, Noonie or the Pope could've invited her for all I cared, as long as she went home with me that night. But my little coal black hair senorita is so pissed at me right now, I don't feel confident that she'll come back to me.

Last night started off so perfect. After our fuckapade down by the waterfall, we decided to continue our epic journey in our bedroom. That's right, *our* bedroom. Because I moved up in that bitch the first night seeing her. At the time the north wing sheltered five women and one man. (Carmen and Shyamae' hadn't moved here yet.)

Later that night after Maria rode my ass to sleep, I woke up sweating and panting like I'd just ran a marathon. I remember hearing Maria ask was I alright and the next thing I know I was fucking for dear life. Right before she boarded the yacht, her last words to me was, "Fuck you sideways bitch!"

That does not sound like the love of my life coming back to be with me.

As the hours passed, I found myself falling into a deep sleep. I remember dreaming about howling wolves........ I awoke with a start and saw my brothers looking in the same direction as our Chief. Tatum stood from his sleeping bag and made his way down the trail before ducking off into the deep forest. I was up and running with my brothers in toe. I came to a stop in an open field right behind Tatum. Karden bumped into me, causing me to come further out in the open. That's when I saw what Tatum was seeing.

In the center of the field was a pack of wolves under the pale white moon, mating. But this wasn't just *any* animal mating ritual. This shit was literally vicious.

The one that stood out the most was this huge gray wolf who'd just ripped the throat out of a tan bitch he'd just got through fucking. It was obvious he was the Alpha. A white wolf came from the east end of the forest into the clearing when the gray wolf spotted her. The white wolf walked in circles around the pack orgy as the silver eyes of the gray wolf followed her. I noticed how Tatum was focused on the two. His hazel eyes bore holes into the gray wolf as he made his way to the left side of the clearing where the white wolf stopped. The wolves faced each other. They were so close, that if by a hair of an inch, their noses would be touching. Then....oh....so....slowly, the gray wolf began to walk circles around the bitch. She never gave chase, which is odd because most female wolves do.

After the gray wolf's third circle, he stopped right behind her tail. After she raised it a little, it wasn't his nose he stuck there.

Three licks.

We all watched as the gray wolf did foreplay on the female. Then he mounted her and she went willingly. Normally a mating session between animals last seconds, maybe sometimes a few minutes tops. But these two was not ordinary wolves. I could actually hear the white wolf's sexual

pants as the gray wolf bit into her flank and began rolling his groin into her rear. Beside me Tatum was panting himself. The faster his breaths came the harder the gray wolf fucked the bitch. Soon all of the wolves were panting, keeping in time with Tatum. I looked over to see his face and bare chest dripping with sweat, his hands clinched into fists, his body stiff as a board. Then in one long breathe he relaxed and all of the wolves released their sighs with his.

The gray wolf slid off the white one. The white wolf laid on her back with her paws up. To my amazement, the gray wolf licked her nozzle, then her belly.

He then faced Tatum and the rest of the wolf pack follow suit. Tatum stepped forward. Each step he took towards them, they took a step of their own towards him.

They never attacked him.

He stared into the silver eyes of the gray wolf as he patted his head. The rest of the wolves surrounded him, wanting the same human affection.

"What the fuck Tatum," Karden asked.

Tatum just kept right on interacting with the wolves. After a few more minutes passed, he stood and walked in the middle of the field. As he past them his hand glided across the gray and white wolves heads. When he got directly in the center, he beckon the two forward, where they each took his flanks. The rest of the wolves faced forward and we all focused our attention on him.

He looked at each of his brothers before he spoke. "We have to get the fuck away from here as soon as possible."

"Tatum, what the fuck are you talking about? Who have to leave?"

"Us. The Pack and mates. We cannot stay here."

"What the fuck Tatum? You just became Chief of this Island. We can't leave," Karden said looking to us for help to talk some sense into him.

"Either we leave this island with our mates or we can stay and die with them."

He didn't have to say another word. "I'll start packing."

"Hold on Cole," Tatum said holding up his hand. "Not now, we'll leave soon, after the ceremony tomorrow."

"Fuck that, Tatum," Tyvine said shaking his head. "We need to leave now. Shit like this doesn't happen, unless the girls are around. If that wasn't a sign that we should get the fuck out of here ASAP, I don't know what is. You just had a telepathic orgy with wolves, man! And in the mist of all that fucking, even they told you we need to get away from here."

"I know, but we can't just up and run. We have to tie up some loose ends here and save a brother."

"What do you mean 'save a brother'? If all of us are going, who needs to be saved?" Moham looked at each of us. The fear for his brothers loud and clear in his face.

"The whole pack isn't going. Two will no longer be with us after tomorrow." "Okay, Tatum. You're scaring the shit out of me now. We're saving a brother, but he is also disbanded from our pack?"

"No one here tonight have to worry themselves about being disband. But our younger brothers have been corrupted. Tonight will be their last night as brothers. Tomorrow night, our young brother and his mate will no longer be with us." He said this with unshed tears glistening in his eyes.

"Tatum," Karden asked. What's with the wolves?"

"They are family. These two," he said referring to the two sitting on his left and right, "will remain with us until we need them no more. They bare gifts to heirs."

Okaaay. Whatever that means.

"Anyway, we have to be deemed rulers of this land before we leave. The wedding ceremony *must* take place."

"But what about the "Birthing Ritual?"

I actually saw him shudder before he responded. "The "Birthing Ritual," was intended for women to die during childbirth. No woman will survive it. It was a shock my mother survived the first time."

We were moving slowly, but closer to him and the wolves as we spoke. "But there's no way around it. It's part of our sacred law."

"We'll be back in plenty of time before Jameria gives birth. But for the rest of the women, Jameria has a plan to discard them from the ritual. She was going to wait and tell you after the wedding. So keep it to yourselves." Damn, I love my sister.

"For now, we're staying the rest of the night here, planning for an even longer time away from the island."

"How long?"

"I don't know, but after the "Birthing Ritual," whether Jameria makes it or not, we have to leave, he said. At that moment, I felt his pain when he uttered the words.

Jameria is Tatum's life. His love for her is so strong, that many men have died just from glancing. They both had shed blood for each other many times. That's why I know his finding Jameria was no coincidence. The day we went to get her, there was a weird feeling in the truck. Almost like we were being pulled to her. When I asked Tatum how exactly he knew where to look, I was flabbergasted with his response.

He said, "'I didn't. In North America, back during slavery, it was common for slave owners to take their slaves to bed.

"But Jameria has more than five different linage in her blood.....most of it Indian."

He laughed. "North America Indians were slave owners too."

If my father heard him, he'd kill him. "Impossible. How can you say something like that? Our family bloodline have ruled for centuries. There's nowhere in our records of such blasphemy. Not even in the States!"

"Calm down, man. Back in those times, there were several tribes known to own slaves. Except for one tribe that stood out. The Sioux. They claimed slaves, but they also married them. That's how I found Jameria. I had to start there and trace her bloodline. First it started out as a project for school, until I was told I had to start my own Pack. But the most amazing part of finding her was, when I traced her linage all the way back to the *Pumpush* tribe." Tatum's eyes glowed with the revelation. As if the words were priceless coming from his tongue. And in a way, it was.

The Pumpush tribe was fierce warriors from the jungle. They are known for their stamina and virility. As soon as council heard Jameria was a descendent from the ancient Amazonian tribe, the skies was her limit. There is nothing in this world my sister *cannot* have. And she used it to her advantage, too.

When Motif was still Chief, Tatum and Jameria lied, plotted and even killed to protect our pack. The recent incident was when Motif's pack decided they wanted to try their hand at kidnapping and rape. The smart thing they did that night after Motif's ass whipping was stay the fuck away from Jameria. But the damn fools decided to go after my girl. They thought my little Maria was timid and shy, because of her petite size. Yet, under the baby doll soft lace dresses is ropes of muscle wrapped around her lean steel like bones……..and don't forget the 510 pound silver back gorilla that's always on the built-in patio Jameria had added on to the palace north wing for Maria's friend Bo-Bo, that no one knew was living there, but the pack.

Jameria and Tatum was having dinner with Carmen, Pierce, and his father Elder Marlease. Tyce, Moham, and Kalanie was in Cougar's rooms playing with Sasha's new litter. I was in Kelanie's sitting room whipping Karden's ass in *Madden*, when something slammed hard against the door. After a moment of shock, we were both on our feet, heading to the door. With my hand on the knob, a screeching cry, halted me from turning that lock. The cry was so horrific, it chilled me to the bone. A man was screaming, crying, begging for someone to please open the door and let them in, while in the background other voices was begging for forgiveness and asking God to save them or help them as their voices was being cut off right after each loud bang in the hall. Karen and I both stood there like fools staring at the damn door. The phone ringing in the bedroom finally got Karden's feet loosen from the floorboards.

"Hello? Cougar? What the hell is going on out there," he said still staring at the sitting room door. "What? Is she alright?"

"What? What's going on Karden?" Something told me that I didn't want to hear his next words.

"It's Cougar. Hold on." He put it on speakerphone and place the receiver back on the hook.

"Hello? Karden, you there?"

"Yeah, Cole's here too. Repeat what you just said."

"Kelanie's hanging outside my bedroom window with a big ass bird talking about Maria and a monster....The damn bird said we should stay in here until the monster leaves. But that's not my problem. *My* problem is, I think Maria's monkey jammed my damn door, now I can't get out!"

I ran out the bedroom to the door, not realizing all the screaming and banging had stopped. As soon as I snatched it open, I closed it back.

Karden stared at me with a lifted brow. I took a deep breath and opened the door again, but slowly. The entire north wing hall was covered in blood, bones, brains, and intestines stewed everywhere. A man's hand was still on the outer doorknob. God only knows where the rest of him was. A couple of doors down Tyvine and Moham finally broke through the piles of bodies that had Cougar's door jammed. And standing in the middle of the mayhem was my beautiful sweet Maria.

Most of the body parts had on military gear. The two bodies Maria left whole was Motif's first and second in command from his retired pack.

"I hope the Chief and Mistress don't be too mad I messed up the new carpet," she said sighing. "They just had it done."

After *that* incident, we should've left.

Chapter 5

Pierce............

I'm in hell. Scratch that. It will be hell to pay if the Pack ever finds out me and Boaz ran a train on Noonie. I can't believe that bitch tried to set Tatum up. She probably did it thinking Boaz was the father. I'm still trying to figure out how the fuck something like this happened, since we both used condoms. But like Bo said, "'She probably poked holes in them before she put them on us.'"

Shit had really got out of hand, when she first came to us on the beach talking about she's with child.

I almost fainted.

Until she said, she'll take care of it.

Me and Boaz thinking, 'Cool. She's going to have an abortion.' But, instead of this bitch having the damn thing abominated, she decides to pin the shit on somebody else. Unfortunately, for Noonie, she lost the baby in the fight with Jameria.

As soon as she got off the boat, Jameria told me and Bo to let Tatum know about the meeting after their wedding ceremony. I had a feeling it was something bad since Demarcus had the same expression Jameria wore.

On our way to let the brothers know, the women had returned, I had to ask, "Do you think she knows?"

"Yes," he said. "Rumors were already circulating before they left yesterday. Of course Demarcus gave her all of the juicy details."

"Do you think Noonie told anyone that it was one of us, who got her pregnant?"

"I don't know. Probably not......unless she was trying to get rid of Carmen or Shyamae'. But I think she's going to try to go after Jameria since she fucked-up her plans with Tatum."

Before we made it to the ceremonial courtyard, we could smell the strawberry, peach, and brown sugar candles scenting the air. We walked down the center of the royal blue satin aisle that will soon be filled with purple rose petals and around the white enormous rose podium to the grooms room, where Cole just exit from.

"Hey, I was just coming to check on you guys. Is everything okay," he said, now dressed in pearl white worm silk woven loose fitting slacks with matching robe. The only jewelry that adorned his muscled body was the two karat diamonds in each ear and the royal gold swathe with the Pack's emblem draped across his bare chest.

"Yeah. The girls just made it and the guest are lined at the entrance…… Jameria called an emergency meeting after the ceremony."

He looked puzzled for a moment, but then saw the guest was starting to take their seats and told us to go get ready.

~~~

As I stood at the podium in my bronze silk attire with the rest of my brothers, my eyes scanned the audience until they clashed with Noonie's. When Boaz walked Shy down the aisle, Noonie stopped him mid-way to plant a kiss on his cheek, then whispered something in his ear. He'd snatched his arm away and hurried down the aisle to his mate. Carman asked me what that was all about, but I just shrugged my shoulders, still thinking of a way to tell her I fucked up.

Just when I was about to whisper to Bo, the wedding song began to play. The entire audience stood to watch the rest of the Pack mates enter as bridesmaids to the bride. But to their surprise all five of my sisters walked out in wedding gowns with Elder Demarcus in the middle holding Jameria and Kelanie's hands.

Tatum, Cole, Karden, Tyvine, and Moham stood out to receive their brides and hear the gasps and mummers echo in the open air of the garden. I could actually smell the hate coming off of Motif's skin. Everyone in the audience was in a state of shock. Instead of one, there will be five marriages happening tonight.

Carmen and Shy stood as their bridesmaids and me and Bo, stood as best men to our brothers.

The sisters were beautiful.

Cougar rocked a diamond studded sleeveless white gown. The slit from high thigh to heel made the dress more alluring than meant for an actual wedding. Next to Cougar, Kelanie graced the ceremony as if it was a runway with her own sleeveless gown. The long cream sheath enhanced her cleavage by a cluster of diamonds that not only supported her dress, but also highlighted her figure.

Beautiful Maria wore a very soft looking sheer wedding gown that was elegant and conservative in the front, but the sway dipped very low in the back made the appeal dangerous.

Tyce, next to Maria, had on a flattering traditional white off the shoulder gown with a floral train is romantic, but the cut out back makes quite a statement. But it was Jameria's gown that stood out.

It looked as if it was painted on her body. She wore a beautiful soft gold slim gown that complimented her hour glass figure. It shimmered in the noonday sun with tiny crushed diamonds setting off a soft glow. The sweetheart cleavage molded perfectly to her 36C cup mounds. Her hair was pinned in loose curls on top of her head with a chocolate diamond hair comb to match her honey brown eyes. The two baby snakes so strategically wrapped in her hair, you would think they were designed as part of her outfit.

Demarcus holding her hand as if it was a rare jewel itself, was sporting an elegant tailor maid tux. Huge diamonds glittering from his ears, wrists, and hands. His long hair was hanging down for a change. With a part down the middle, he looks a lot like Cole does now. Tatum also shares some of those features.

The crowd was shaking their heads and applauding in amazement as five of my pack brothers received their brides.

For two weeks our pack family worked hard to pull this off without Motif's knowledge. Jameria and Tatum made arrangements with Moham, Tyvine, and Karden's fathers to meet and discuss the future of their sons. That meeting only lasted thirty minutes (with only a little hesitation from Mara). They were euphoric.

Meanwhile, the rest of us went about delivering invitations, decorating, and getting fitted for our outfits. All of this taking place while Motif and Noonie was in recovery. By the time they was able to receive the public, Tatum and Jameria's wedding was in the air. The rest of the brides and grooms was kept on the hush, hush......the only gift Jameria requested from Council.

Boaz and I watched as ten of our brothers and sisters stood in front of the priest as he began prayer. I looked over to Carmen. Her thick long lashes casted a shadow over the light brown skin of her high cheekbones, giving the appearance her lovely eyes were closed, until those black orbs met mine. She smiled and winked, making silly faces to get me to smile.

It worked.

Carmen and Shy were beautiful, also. The off shoulder bronze sarong fitted snuggly or that's the suggestion it's giving. The low dip in the back of the dress, gave the illusion of a sheath being draped over the body, while the front looked as if I was drawn on their bodies, showing off curves that makes me so proud to be a part of this Pack.

Though Carmen and I have been intimate more times than I can count, it still amazes me that someone so beautiful can actually belong to me. So when we encountered a problem with Bo and Shy, I thought I could save Carmen and I both if I just accept the proposition Noonie offered and the whole thing would be over, but instead I was screwed.

The bitch told us all of our brothers had to do it when they reached the age of sixteen. I knew it was a lie, but Bo said it was the last time. Yet, he and Shy were making plans for us later tonight after our brothers left.

I don't know what to do. If I tell Tatum everything that's been happening, he'll kick me out for sure. Probably kill us. But if I don't, I could risk losing Carmen forever, because of Bo and Shy and their forceful advances. The ceremony went by real quick, because the Priest knew what to expect, making sure not to ask, 'Do anyone object to these unions?'

Jameria cried.

But instead of tears of happiness, it was more like tears of frustration. Tatum and Demarcus looked pissed as well. I could actually hear Cole growling under his breath. I was just as confused as the rest of my pack family.

As soon as the Priest said, 'You may kiss your brides,' Tatum and Jameria didn't waste any time getting to the grooms dressing room. All of us went, wondering what in the hell happened now.

"How did they find you?!" When we entered, Tatum was already pacing the floor.

"I don't know. I don't think they were trying to find me, either. I think someone went and found them," she said looking at her new husband's now frozen stance.

He faced her and stared deep into her eyes.

Just then, Elder Demarcus entered the room and went straight to Jameria, pulling her into his embrace. "Are you okay? We'll have them thrown off the island immediately," he said eyeing Tatum.

Karden stepped forward. "Whatever is going on, please tell us, because right now I'm lost. Is someone after you Mistress?"

Demarcus, Tatum, Cole, and Jameria, just stared at him.

"What did I say?"

Tatum spoke. "Jameria's mother *and* father was at the ceremony."

The room was completely quiet.

Cougar broke first. "How in the hell did something like *this* happen? We already have enough shit to deal with."

79

"It doesn't matter how it happened. They're leaving now, Demarcus said trying to march out of the room.

Jameria caught him by his arm. "We need to discuss something else with the Pack." Demarcus was relaxed, but his anger didn't decrease. Jameria returned to her seat next to the blue stained glass window. "Noonie miscarried. She was pregnant when we fought. She's claiming the child was a pack member's, but she haven't released a name."

Tyvine burst out laughing. "That bitch wasn't pregnant. No man is stupid enough to crawl between those legs. And anyway do you really think any of us would do something like that," he said as his laughter changed a little to being annoyed.

"That's the point Tyvine. She *was* pregnant. The doctor confirmed it because I made sure to get a second and third opinion. We know it's not Motif's. All male officials have to get a vasectomy at age thirty-five, she said.

During the entire discussion, the more Tatum looked at us, the angrier he became. Or was it my imagination.

"Well, I don't give a fuck what she say. It wasn't us. Tatum you should banish that bitch. Even after that ass whipping of trying to set *you* up, she still haven't learned shit," Cole said.

"Calm down son. No matter what she tells anyone, they won't believe her anyway. After the results of the blood test, she won't have a choice but to leave."

After Demarcus revelations, it took everything in me to keep from dropping to my knees. God, what has Bo gotten us into?

"We can't dwell on it now. Just thought you should know. Anyway, we have a reception to attend. After all of you return from your honeymoons, this thing with Noonie should be resolved. Now let's go meet mommy and daddy," Demarcus said, his anger returning.

"Boaz, Pierce. I want to talk to you two for a moment," Tatum said. The rest of the Pack left the room without a word. Only Shy hesitated, looking confused.

As soon as Moham closed the door behind him, Tatum had us pinned against the wall by our throats. Struggling was useless. I used my time trying to meditate and hold the air I had left in my head as long as I could, before I passed out.

"I can tell you two mothafucka's been busy," he said between clenched teeth. He tighten his grip and I just couldn't take it anymore.

I started to struggle. He loosen his grip, dropping me to the floor like a rag doll. "Tatum please....we-"The deep growl that was rumbling in his heaving chest, was now more pronounced. I looked up to see Boaz eyes rolling into the back of his head.

I didn't think, just reacted.

I tackled Tatum from below, sending him to the ground. Then, I wheeled around and threw Boaz six foot two inch frame over my shoulder and rushed out of the door, without the thought of looking back.

By the time we made it to the only linen closet with a lock, Bo was still trying to get his breathing under control. "Man……he's going….to kill us," he manage to get out.

"We have to tell Jameria." He knew what I meant. This thing with Noonie might ruin our Pack. And to be honest Bo and Shy both, need psychological evaluation about their sexual habits. "She can help us."

"Are you crazy!? Noonie still haven't healed all the way from an ass whippin that happened two weeks ago. Imagine what she would do to us!"

"She'll be upset with us, but she's understanding. My father told

me a woman who shows no pain, he'll put his life in her hands

any day. He told me to always bet on Jameria, because she will do the right thing no matter what," I said peeping out of the keyhole.

When I turned back he had this strange look on his face. He quickly snapped out of it, shaking his head. "I don't know man. You see the way Tatum is. And Jameria would kill or die for him without question."

"I know. He growled. He has never in his life done anything like that….well, at least not at one of us. Moham said something happened to them in the woods. He said Tatum was more

82

affected by it than they were.""That explains the two wolves I saw lounging in their chambers this morning," he said standing.

"Are you able to make it? We need to get to Jameria."

"I'm straight, but I really think you're wasting your time going to her for help."

I stared at him a moment. I thought as Jameria's left hand Bo would *want* to go to the Mistress for help. He's as close to her as Tatum is....or at least he's supposed to be.

After peeping around every nook and cranny we finally made our way to the reception that's being held smack in the middle of the palace courtyard. The Pack was lined up to make their entrance, But Tatum and Karden was nowhere in sight. Jameria turned as we approached her.

"Mistress we need to talk to you immediately."

"No need Pierce. I already know what you and Boaz did. We'll talk about it later in private. For now I suggest you get in line," she said facing the audience.

Just then Tatum appeared from somewhere behind us." Are you boys alright," he said eyeing Bo.

I didn't say a word.

I made my way to the back of the line where my eyes met Carmen's. She didn't have to say anything. I knew the shit Boaz was study getting us into was killing her inside. She was at a breaking point. I tried to grab her hand and she snatched it away, looking straight ahead as if I wasn't there. Boaz on the other hand received a different reaction. Shyamae' slapped the shit out of him. I didn't even see it coming.

Jameria glanced back and asked her, "Are you done?"

"No."

"Then you'll have to put your frustrations off until after the reception. Put your lady face back on. We're about to receive the public."

 And just like that, the females morphed from mad pissed off bitches, to happy young ladies, ready for the world.

Chapter 6

Boaz........

Fuck me sideways. And that's exactly what Noonie did to our asses. I let that bitch double cross *me*. Instead of her stupid ass sticking with the plan to record Pierce and me fucking her to use against Tatum as a negligent Chief, she double crosses me by putting holes in the damn condoms, still trying to find a way to get Tatum between her legs.

Dumbass cunt.

But it's not her fault she's a lying, conniving, hoe. That bitch been dense since birth. My problem is, I put trust in a stupid person and now I might be dead within a second if the Mistress knows anything about my meeting with Motif. I'd rather it be Jameria anyway.

If Jameria kill me it would be deadly, but silent. But Tatum on the other hand is a beast. He don't just kill, he mutilates your body, then feed it to the snakes before taking your last breath. I watched first-hand how crazy he can get.

It was one night during a full moon, right after him and Jameria met with Motif and Noonie for dinner. He'd caught Motif's head guard, Carvus following them to Jameria's suite. I was on my way to the beach, when I spotted them.

Poor Carvus didn't know my brother well enough. Instead of him tracking my brother, Tatum was baiting him in. That's the first lesson you learn when hunting. Planting the bait for your kill.

He pushed Jameria through the north hall gates and told her he'll be back in a minute. I saw him remove his shirt and tuck it behind a bush by the north wing entrance. I ducked off behind the banquette hall where I could get a better view from the moonlight. When Tatum made it to the bush Carvus was hiding behind, he just kept on walking. Carvus thought the coast was clear to leave, until Tatum popped up behind him like a ghost in a bad dream. I say dream and not nightmare because his dance of death is just too beautiful to even consider a nightmare.

Capoeira is an art him and Jameria mastered together. When they train, it's like an intense sensual dance between intimate lovers. But apart…….

Tatum clipped the man's throat damaging his windpipe right before he broke both of the man's legs. The poor guy never had the chance to scream. He then proceeded to throw the man's body over his shoulder and headed for the woods. No doubt to present Jade with the gift.

Jade is Jameria's anaconda with the emerald green eyes and shiny black scales known as the *titanic boa.* From the time Jameria moved here, Jade has always been the largest snake she trusted on the island. But over the years, she's taking a liking to Tatum and Tyvine from all the people they delivered to her who now adorned the rising 'missing persons list.'

Tatum's Chief now. And only God knows what he'll do next. He ordered the entire Pack's bags to be packed and ready for departure the same night of the reception. We had no idea that included: Pierce, Carmen, Shy, Rubae, uncle Demarcus, and myself. "Whatever problems we have now, will be here when we get back. Right now, I just want to get my family as far away from this place, with the little time we're spared," he said.

We were headed to Tibet. We made a detour to our private landing strip in the States where I thought the extras were to get off. Instead all the happily married couples descended the plane. During the ride Jameria and Tatum spoke quietly but intensely with uncle Demarcus. As she handed him a sheet of paper, I saw tears weld up in Demarcus eyes. He shifted and planted a soft kiss on his beloved daughter's cheek, before she stood and left the plane, pulling me along with her.

I went willingly.

"Bo, I want to talk to you for a minute alone," she said beside me, walking hand-in-hand. Any other else time, this little moment would've been ideal, but after all the shit I did on the island, I really need to be watching for cobra's coming out of her hair. "Bo I know what you and Pierce did with Noonie........and what you and Shy was doing on the island with the other women."

I figured as much, but at least she don't know the worst part. Yet, she was still able to sense the slight discomfort. "Yes Bo, I know about the other women. But that's a subject between you and your mate. My only concern is the conversation you had with Motif about making you Chief."

Shit! Oh shit!!! Shit! Shit! Shit! Shit!

She knew *everything*. The only person I told was Shy. And I knew she wasn't going to say anything, because she's all for me becoming Chief. Hell, the bitch even made plans how she was going to have the whole palace redone once she's Mistress.

Jameria turned to me with all of her bronze beauty glowing in the moonlight. "I'm surprised you would actually do something like this to Tatum," she said with a little admiration. "But a challenge is a challenge. And I don't give a fuck about you being his little brother. From what I see, you're playing grown man games. You and your bitch don't need to hide behind Motif. I'll make it easy for you. Tatum and I decided to send you and your mate on to Tibet to train with the monks. At least after your training, the fight will be fair when we kill you," she said with her perfectly white smile.

As bad as I wanted to know how she found out, I knew it would be the biggest mistake of my life. So I asked another question instead. "Does this mean I'm nolonger a part of the pack?" She looked at me flabbergasted. "Boaz, after all the people you and your mate fucked all over the island, I'd say you been disconnected from this pack months ago. Plus, you're weak minded."

"All because I followed the traditional book? You can't punish me for that. It's not my fault. I stand as your left hand and we're no closer than we were the moment you came here. I'm supposed to be just as close to you as Tatum, but you wouldn't let no one else in. If I go to Council and tell them you had not once laid with me, you'll be exiled."

She stared at me with blank eyes. Her face was too eased. Did she know?

"You didn't know, did you?"

At first I thought she wasn't going to answer. Then she said, "You should've read the fine print. You're not yet eighteen and Demarcus granted Shy permission to date only you." She shook her head at me. "Sorry Bo, but there's no way I'll let that thing hanging between your legs penetrate these walls. But I tell you what, keep fucking with me, there will be no need for training."

I backed down. She's right though. If I go to Council with this, they'll say I voided the contract with Demarcus first. I fucked up so bad. And the fact I hurt my brother beyond repair is leaving a nasty taste in my mouth.

"What about Pierce and Carmen," I said now knowing why my other brother hadn't said bye to me, before climbing into the other plane with the rest of the pack. He also, haven't looked at me since the reception. Being isolated from my two closest brothers was never in my plans.

"What about them? They're apart of us and has nothing to do with the bullshit you two have gotten yourselves into," she said gesturing toward Shy. Even if you decide not to fight us, you two are still no longer apart of this pack." She looked at Shyamae' as she stood to the side with our luggage. "Enjoy your trip." Then she turned and boarded the plane with the rest of her brothers and sisters.

Uncle Demarcus and Rubae' were our companions for the rest of this trip. It was when we made it to Europe, I got fed up.

We headed straight for the Range Rover parked on the strip. "Come on guys. It's getting late and I want to get an early start first thing in the morning."

Over the years, Jameria and Tatum made investments to better suit our lifestyle. They bought several shops, penthouses, apartment complexes, flats, and several sport cars, just to name a few. The long drive to our flats had me bored and focusing on the shit Jameria informed me of and all the people Shy and I bedded for power and pleasure.

My mate and I have done a lot of things together, including women. So when the news hit her that I'd fucked Noonie, she wasn't mad I betrayed her. She was just upset I didn't invite her.

And that's why I love her so much. She wants what I want.

Money and Power with our names in lights.

Those were our main discussions during my visits to her birth home. How to obtain it and keep it. By me being a Chief's son does not guarantee me those riches all the time. Especially now that Tatum's Chief. Before he became Chief, he would put me on a punishment for some little trivial thing I did by taking away my spending allowance and giving it to the fucking slums.

I got fed up at the age of twelve when he tried to pull that bullshit. I lost my virginity that day and never looked back. It was with my tutor, Ms. Veel, the North American exchange student and the diplomat's wife of our island, Mrs. Motuse. The sexy twenty-five year old from the Tayan Island. She lived in Amsterdam and worked on the strip for three years before coming back home. The things she learned........

She fucked me royally.

Taught me things that got me hooked for life.

Shyamae' was no different.

The bitch lives off promises and will do anything to get to the top. Five months before she was due to come live on the island, was my final visit and the day I found out who she really was by a request she made. She wanted to fuck this guy she'd been dating since grade school. The only problem was, her mate had to be her first. Tatum wasn't the only one who could manipulate rules. The next day after I fucked Shyamae' into kingdom come, she called my hotel room asking for me to participate in a threesome. I waxed my dick in her mouth for about an hour, before she told me to finish what her so called boyfriend started. He stood to the side working his seven inches with his hand, while I plummet my eleven inches in her ass to the hilt. "'That's right baby....work that dick.'"

Once she made it the island, it was on.

We fucked the entire Leading Ladies Tea function one night. Bitches knew about us way before Shy was introduced to

Council. That night I fucked at least ten women. Shyamae' had me beat by eating out six women and finger fucking thirteen and she still ended up fucking me, talking about she was a long way from being satisfied. And true to her word, one man is never enough for Shy. So many times, I caught her ass staring at Tatum after training. Even in her fucking dreams, she plays with her pussy moaning his name. You would think shit like that getting in my head, but the fact that I want to fuck my brother's wife makes it even.

From the first day I laid eyes on Jameria, I wanted to fuck her. Slim muscled waist, thirty-six C plump breast, tone round ass, flexible long legs, and full lips I dream about wrapped around my dick every night. But Tatum and Jameria is so closed minded, it was never a consideration taking on other bed partners. But like she said, I'm not of age....yet. She can't be serious about kicking me out of the pack. Who else would she pick as her left hand? I'm closer to those snakes than anybody else in the pack.

"Here's our stop," Demarcus announced.

We went straight to our flat. Like Tatum, Demarcus didn't cut his eyes at me once.

"How the fuck did they find out, Bo," Shy said once we entered our flat.

"Common sense, dumbass. Jameria got snakes crawling all over the palace. Plus, Tatum is starting to catch onto his gift also. I mean the mothafucka actually had wolves guarding Jameria's

92

bedroom. Unchained at that. Then you have Demarcus and his personal spies……..it could be a number of things."

"First let me address that dumbass part. Because if you was so smart, you would've seen Noonie setting your *dumbass* up. And don't forget Pierce punk ass. He was right up in that room with you, but nobody's on him about shit. He left you hanging. And if you ever call me dumb again I'ma drown your ass. Hear me?"

If I had the mind to, I would provoke her further, since my favorite turn-on is her anger. But this bitch is a different kind of crazy and if I start her up, we'll never get out of here.

She changed from her traveling outfit to a black leather mini, thigh high boots, a curly lace front wig, and a purple low-cut top. Then she pulled out her diamond back cigarette case, popping a couple of shrooms in her mouth and passing me two.

"Might as well enjoy it while you can. Since your brother decided he'd rather see you dead, than Chief of Gerillian Island. There's only one option….we have to kill him."

"Don't start that shit again, Shy. You're letting that crap Motif shouting get into your head. I already told you, I'm trying to do all I can to keep from shedding blood. Killing my brother was not an option."

"You said was."

"What," I said facing her.

"You said killing your brother *was* not an option. Is it an option now, Boaz?"

It wasn't an option, until Jameria guaranteed I wasn't hitting that. "I have no other choice," I said stuffing several packets of condoms in my pocket."

She looked me up and down. "You're not going to change?"

I was still wearing my cream knit traveling attire. They're much comfortable than expensive jeans and button down shirts.

Ignoring Shy's question, I grabbed her hand and headed straight to the lobby, asking for our personal car to be brought around. I bought me a brand new Bugatti here in Europe, when the Pack was invited to attend a private luncheon given by the Duke himself. His daughter told me about a private club while I was fucking her in her father's plush office.

I call it the 'Bed Club.' A private European hot spot for the high "freaky" society. Three big ass bomb shelters built underground during that stupid war when Einstein married his first cousin. One shelter was mainly for drinking and partying, but it was the two shelters connected to the back of the bar is what gives the club its appeal. Several king size beds in different silk padded sectionals, was its own décor against the steel walls. The entire green silk padded floor felt like a feathered pillow beneath my feet as we entered the glass enclosed room behind the bar.

The waitress scanned our club card and showed us to our group.

The best investment I ever made. Before you can join this club, a blood test and three thousand (non-refundable), is only the first step. Even after the physical, you still have to be accepted into the club by at least one of the eight group leaders. Its twenty-four members in our group. We don't all meet at the same time. It's a 'whoever is there, is there' type of thing. Here in Europe Shyamae' and I decided to keep it quiet, so we fucked people in our age group only.

Once we made it to our mammoth size bed, five regulars were already there. Three local chic's and the eighteen year old twin Australian males named Levi and Devin, who's attending art school here. The two like other kids in our group, have the type of parents who give them shit loads of money and never ask what's being done with the funds. As long as they don't bother them. The one name Levi had a chic juggling his balls on her tongue at the foot of the bed, while Devin worked a girl in the missionary position and eating out another one at the other end of the bed. Of course it was Devin with pussy in his face. That's the only way we could tell them apart without them mentioning their names. My own mate told me I didn't hold a candle to Devin's tongue action.

Before I made it to the bed good, the blond sitting on Devin's face, came over and started rubbing my dick. I hurriedly put my hair in a ponytail, refusing to let anyone put their hands in my shit. There's no way in hell I'm nasty enough to watch a bitch play with someone else's balls, then put their nasty ass hands in my head. Shit just not going to happen.

Shy had already replaced CeCe (the blond), over Devin's face. CeCe was already on her knees receiving my first nut in her mouth, while I finger fucked the brunette riding Levi, in the ass.

Ginger (the brunette) was kind of dry, so after my second nut I got up and put my tongue in her ass. She was so tight, that if I didn't know any better, I'd say she was never penetrated there before. I got the oil out of Shy's bag, and lubed her up real good, then shoved two fingers deep in her ass. After beating it in for a while, I decided she was open enough to receive me. The problem was Levi's short dick was drying her out fast. It's different when Pierce was my partner in the same bitch. Two big dicks in the same bitch creates, a hell of a lot of friction. Gives a whole new meaning to the word 'gangbang.'

Ginger is a squirter.

Once she got off Levi's dick, I caught Shy's eye and beckon her over so we could do our thing. I pulled Ginger up in my arms with her facing Shy. First stop was shoving her tongue down Ginger's throat while shoving all four of her fingers up the girl's pussy, which instantly drenched us all. I laid on my back, pulling Ginger with me and allowing Shy to do what she do best. She ground her hairless pussy against Ginger's, making my already hard dick swell to an unimaginable proportion. While I came in Ginger's ass for the second time, I let Shy have a turn at me after Ginger squirted in her mouth a couple of times. She leaned forward, kissing me. Her tongue was wet and thick, causing an instant hard-on again. Shy replaced her ass with her mouth, ending the night with me cumming on two beautiful women. After we took a quick shower, we got back in our ride and headed straight for the airport.

Fuck uncle Demarcus.

If him and Tatum want me to do as they say, they're going to have to pay me to do that shit. I had already planned to dip from the scene for a little, while Motif go along with his plan to get Jameria and her spawn off the island, leaving me to come back to challenge Tatum for Chief of Gerillian. Motif guaranteed me there was no way Tatum can win if he is too grief stricken from Jameria leaving. Knowing how he truly feels about her, gives me the advantage. Jameria is Tatum's only weakness.

We made it to the airport in record time, catching the 4:30 flight out. After we do a couple of flight changes, our final destination is Texas. South Padre' Island is where we will lay low while Motif takes care of his part of the plan with Jameria parents. Or hopefully by the time he sends for us, Jameria will be dead from child birth and Tatum will be so fucked up in the head from her death, that he will hate the bastard child that will take his beloved wife. The only part of this plan I hate, is I didn't get to fuck Jameria.

I wanted her for so long. I didn't comprehend until I got up in age that she considered me more as a child, than someone she could actually be with. The week before my fourteenth birthday, the day I was going to make my move, was too horrific to put into words. I practiced that entire day, how I was going to approach her and let her know how I felt. I didn't need a mate. I just wanted her.

The locks had just been installed for her sitting room and it was Kelanie's first night on the island. She was staying in her den/guestroom during her training. The curtains were pulled over the glass enclosed area. When I approached Jameria's door to knock, that's when my world changed.

Her soft moans and little cries of pleasure drew my curiosity to the bedroom keyhole. There, lying on the custom made king size bed, with her beautiful body glistening from the moonlight through the windowpane, was Jameria with her body wrapped around Tatum's body so tight, it was hard to tell where she began and he end. I knew then I never had a glimpse of a chance with her. Tatum's dick was humongous and Jameria took that shit with ease. Grabbing his ass cheeks, grinding pelvis to pelvis, skin to skin. "Squeeze me tighter," he said. Pure pleasure was written all over his face.

Sweat poured of their bodies in pools. Rocking into each other in a slow rhythm to *"Forever"* by 8Ball & Mjg, featuring Lloyd.

Un-fucking-believable.

Her fingers rotated in his hair, bringing his mouth to hers as her tongue snaked out between his waiting lips. He slowly removes himself from between her captured legs and crawls off the bed. She follows. He grips the bed post with his right hand and place a pillow on the floor between his legs. She placed her hand in his as she eased on her knees. First licking around the engorged head, then oh so slowly, her lips glided down his length, not stopping until her lovely face was buried in the black curls between his legs. As Tatum's right hand tightened around the post, his left hand snaked into her long thick hair, gripping a handful and grinding her face hard against his pelvis. And if I didn't believe it without seeing it, I would call anyone else a lie, but that big dick mothafucka started pounding his dick in her mouth, like he's beating up the pussy.......And she was enjoying that shit!

Tatum's hips began rotating faster as he sandwiched Jameria's head between the side of the bed and his thighs. I could hear the deep growl within him as his body trembled from the powerful release. But my nightmare was far from over. As Jameria drank the last of his seed, the mothafucka got hard all over again. He lifted her off her knees and over his head as she did a full split, exposing a thick fat hairless pussy. She'd wrapped her legs around Tatum's head, after he literally started fucking her with his tongue. She rained on his ass, leaving his long hair drenched in her juices. I prayed that she drowned his ass.

The whole time that damn song was on repeat and whenever it hit that part about "'I know you want to fuck my hoe,'" my heart fell. Every time she trembled from his touch, my heart skipped beats, knowing I'll never touch that. After her umpteenth nut, he laid her back on the bed, their tongues in a battle to dominate the other's mouth, their bodies reconnecting. Then he rose up over her and began pounding into her like a beast. Growling, biting into her flesh and the whole time Jameria was in heaven, and screaming how much she loved him.

That's when I decided if she want that motherfucker, she can die with his ass, because when I got older, I would become Chief. Motif had been trying for years to get me to turn against my brother. The surprised look on his face when I walked into his office to take him up on his offer, will last me a life time. Though,

I never told him why I changed my mind, he figured it out when I told him my most important demand was that I wanted to fuck Jameria. I was supposed to have *been* hit that, but Tatum was always on guard and that selfish ass bitch I got as a mate, always wanted to taste Jameria's pussy, so that plan fell through. So I said fuck the pussy and decided to stick with my plan to become Chief.

Once I told Shy what was up, she came up with her own shit which lead us roping Pierce and Carmen into our plan, unwilling. Carmen was easy and too trusting. Shy invited her to my suite to study for a test. By the time she finished a whole glass of tea Shyamae' spiked, she was open to the world.......and wet too. Carmen is a squirter.

She's the one who turned me onto them.

The first time I fucked her, I practically bathed in her juices. Each time I thrust up in her as she rode me, her body was like a fountain of cream soaking me down to the crack of my ass. Yeah, she was easy, but Pierce was another story. Like Tatum, he thought his pole was made for one chic, but I quickly enlightened him. I let Shy turn his ass out. But due to the fact they were tricked or forced or whatever word they chose to use, had them thinking I'm supposed to take the blame for every-fucking-thing. Either way, we all came, so Pierce and Carmen can't say they didn't enjoy that shit!

Chapter 7

Demarcus............

"Jameria. Boaz just left........Yeah. He did exactly what you said he would do. Okay, Luv. I'll meet you back at the palace in a few months, Love you. Bye."

"How is she," Rubae' asked, lounging on the couch, making kissy faces at the young viper nestled around her forearm. Jameria left the baby reptiles behind for me to babysit.

"She and the baby are doing just fine."

A couple of days before the guys were due back from their hunt, Jameria came to me crying and mad as hell. The tears was a surprise, but telling me what's on her mind was never a problem.

"'Dad, I'm pregnant and I'm going to kill Tatum,'" she said to me, once she could form coherent words, that is.

"'Jameria, you cannot kill Tatum because you were irresponsible. Blaming him because you forgot to take your pills a few times is not your style.'" Once Rubae' pried the girl's hands from around my throat, I was able to catch my breath and listen to her after she calmed down.

"'Tatum switched my birth control pills for fertility pills,'" she said tossing me the pack of fake birth control pills. "I've been taking those damn things since you two let for your trip.'"

After hearing her revelations of how Tatum made the fertility pills look like birth control pills, how he planned the trip for Rubae' and I to take a small vacation to separate us, so his evil little plan could follow through…..which it did, I must add. I decided to let my great nephew take his ass whipping like a man. Though Tatum is wrong for what he did, I understand why he did it. When I first met Jameria, I always knew being a wife and mother was the furthest thing from her mind. Bowing down to someone other than herself was ludicrous. But Tatum is just as strong willed and pigheaded as she is. Yet, the new problems that accumulated since they became the new leading couple have the two running the island like the queen and king, I know they can be.

The arrival of Ella D. Beau and Boseur Tante was the worst vengeance Motif brought upon this family. The damned couple was not together, but they are *working* together. As soon as we exited the groom chambers to attend the reception, they attacked Jameria at the door. Hugging and kissing her like she was a returning kidnapped victim they've been looking for, for decades. And my beautiful daughter knew exactly who the fools were, but she played along just the same.

Pushing the pale petite woman away from her, she asked, "'Do I know you?'"

The woman looked flabbergasted. "'Even after all these years, a child never forgets her mother. It's me Jameria. I'm your mother Ella D.'"

After the admission, the tall dark man, who no doubt was her father, sprung forward, extending his hand. His southern heritage loud and pronounced in his features.

"'And I'm your father Boseur, but everybody calls me Bozy........or dad, if you like.'"

I was so proud when I saw her hand clench into a fist for just that split second.

"'I apologize, but I don't know, have never heard of, or even met you. Pat Ann Beau raised me from birth and not once did she mentioned either of you.'" When they started to protest, she held up her hand, stopping their advances. "'I know you two have a lot to say, but unfortunately for you this is not the conversation I want to have on my wedding day. Now if you would please excuse me, my new husband and I are going to escort my father into the reception garden for this special occasion. You're both are welcome to stay and enjoy the festivities.'" The young vipers that was cordially wrapped in the pile of curls atop her head raised their heads in a striking pose.

Jameria's agitation had just hit its highest point.

The woman took a step back, but the man held his stance. Under his crisp white shirt, two black runners poked their heads out from between the buttons.

I watched in astonishment as the two circled each other. Jameria with snakes twined in her hair and her father with two wrapped around his torso, which was so undistinguished hidden. I then stopped her, by laying a gentle hand on her shoulder.

"'Happy occasion remember?'"

The snakes in her hair relaxed back into their decretive positions and the runners eased their heads back inside his shirt.

They stared each other down for long moments before Tatum showed up and pulled her hand forward. Then she smiled that beautiful sweet smile of hers, the one that earned her the name 'Badb' amongst our people. Meaning a feared serpent goddess. When people sees that smile, they either run or if it's your first time seeing it, you're pulled in by its beauty, paralyzing you before she strikes.

"'I look forward to our conversation. Until we meet again,'" she said as we passed them and entered the reception garden.

"'In due time,'" he replied.

During those few intense moments with her father, Tatum had just enough time to whisper to me that it was urgent that he speak with me alone. After we greeted everyone at the reception, I pulled Tatum into my office before Council made the historical announcement.

"'What's the problem, Tatum,'" I asked as soon as the doors closed. He proceeded to pull me further into the room, heading straight for the bathroom where he cut on the shower, closed and locked the door.

His actions had me a little nervous.

"'Uncle Demarcus, I felt the call of the wolves,'" he'd said.

"'What did you say?'"

"'While you and the girls was on the mainland last night, the guys and I decided to go camping. Sometime after midnight, I woke up from a strange dream........'"

I felt he had more to say concerning his dreams, but from the look in his eyes, I could tell he decided to continue with the story at hand.

"'Anyway, I felt someone calling me.'" I notice he said *felt* instead of *heard*. "'It was so loud and clear that each cry from a wolf felt like it came straight from my heart.'"

By the time he finished the story, I'd already planted myself in a nearby vanity chair, stunned. "'How? From what Jameria told me, the only way for you to obtain the voice is by going to war with the insect people. Whoever the fuck they're supposed to be. Are you telling me that it just called to you and you just received it, like an expected gift you receive for your birthday? It just came to you like that?'" By this time, I'd already had in my head to come up with my own scenario. Hell, the Pack's hidden gifts scares me more than Jameria's. At least she can control hers.

"'Not exactly,'" he said peeping out of the door, then locking it back. "'I don't know how to explain it uncle Demarcus. The only thing I can tell you is after the mating of the wolves, they spoke to me. Told me things I would've never imagine. As soon as the voice came, it was gone again, but not before giving me an important message.'"

Anxiously, I asked, "'What was it?'"

"'To leave and leave the second born behind. Next thing I know images was popping up in my head left and right. It's the recurring one that kept me up late last night.'"

Tatum stood at six foot five inches tall with a chiseled jaw, slim waist, and muscular build. His dark cinnamon skin tone lay in contrast to his light hazel eyes. And a bright white smile that can make a nun drop to her knees. But there are some feathers to my nephew that will have me terrified to even look at.

Whatever the recurring dream was, from the look on Tatum's face, I didn't even *want* to know. But I found myself leaning close asking, "'What was it?'"

"'Boaz attacking Jameria,'" he said choking up. He looked at me with tears in his half crazed eyes. "He had her tied down, mouth gagged, beaten and bruised... "'She was naked,'" he whispered, the tears now streaming down his face. The faraway look in his eyes, let me know it's a nightmare he relives daily.

"'Tatum you're thinking too much of it. It was just a dream. You know Jameria can take care of herself and then some. Her nature is to attack first. Boaz cannot possibly take her on.'"

"'Uncle Demarcus, Jameria's pregnant. After the "Birthing Ritual," she'll be at her weakest point, not to mention what Jameria told me she found out about Boaz and Motif…….All the shit him and Shy been plotting and planning. Trying their best to pull Pierce and his mate in with them. You know if Carmen hadn't come forward, I still would've believed everything the wolves showed me. I know now I never had much faith in my own brother.'" He fell into a chair as if the revelations exhausted him.

Everything Tatum said, all the unanswered questions concerning a few of the leaders of the land. Boaz taking out Jameria after she gives birth. And Shyamae' taking over as Mistress.

"'Tatum, who else knows about the pregnancy?'"

"'Just the pack and you.'"

"'Good and let's keep it that way.......for now. When we get on that plane to leave for your honeymoon, make sure you have enough of everything for you and your pack to sustain you a while. Don't come back here until I say it's okay. Do you hear me?'"

He shook his head in protest. "'No, uncle Demarcus. You have to come with us. You can't come back here. If Motif finds out Jameria's pregnant, he'll stop at nothing to get to her.....including hurting you.'"

"'No Tatum. The Council doesn't know anything yet and Boaz don't know that I know Jameria's pregnant. I'll leave with you long enough until he goes in another direction. There's no way I'm leaving him and Shy here on the island with Motif, while most of the pack is away on their honeymoons. He needs to know that you know everything, so he can make his own choice to disappear for a while.'"

"'I'm ahead of you on that part, but what about you. I don't want you coming back to this island alone uncle Demarcus.'"

"'Don't worry. Me and Rubae' will disappear, too. Just long enough for me to make the necessary transfers to you. You'll have to get new passports-,'" I smiled to myself remembering who I was talking to and the shenanigans him and my daughter use to get into with fake I.D's.

"'We'll get all of that under control uncle Demarcus, but I really want you to come with us,'" he said, as if pleading for the last time.

I looked into my great-nephew eyes (so much like his mother's) and grabbed his smooth face between my hands.

"'Listen to me. Once you leave here, you can*not* come back here for a long time Tatum. Do you understand me? Don't come back,'" I'd said staring directly into his piercing eyes. "'Don't worry about me Tatum. Your main goal is to get Jameria and the pack as far away from this place as possible.'"

The determined glint in his eyes is one of the reasons why Jameria had to be informed immediately. It will have to be her to keep Tatum at bay.

"'The kids will be fine, Luv. Don't look so worried," Rubae' said, breaking my train of chaotic thoughts. She'd place the young vipers back in their cage and had two glasses and a bottle of wine set out on the coffee table with peach scented candles burning with the lights low.

At the age of forty Rubae's lean frame was muscular because of her many daily activities, plus being the private nurse to one of our highest royalties. Her sandy color hair, cut short, enhancing her oval shape face, could easily be mistaken for a twenty year old. The diamond earrings I bought her on her last birthday, sat a soft glow against her tan skin. The silk gown fit snuggly to her slim waist, making her small breast look fuller.

She proceeded to open the bottle of wine as she spoke. "You know Jameria can take care of herself. She's still in the early stages of her pregnancy, and you know Tatum's a little psycho when it comes to her. There's no way anyone will be able to touch her." She passed me a glass before sitting back on the plush sofa with her own.

"It's hard seeing my kids go through so much at the beginning of their adult lives. Now I see why Ky made the decisions she made back then. This is not what I wanted for Jameria and Cole. I wanted them to have *some* kind of freedom or at least normalcy," I said taking a long gulp from the glass.

She took a sip of her wine before sitting it down again, then lean forward and began to message my calves through my black linen slacks. "Do you not see me sitting here looking all sexy for you," she said moving her hands up my thighs.

I threw one leg over the back of the sofa and unbuckled my belt along with my slacks just as she slid between my legs.

"Please forgive me for my rudeness." My dick shot straight up as she caressed my balls through the thin fabric. "Understand nothing like this has ever happened before. I was raised to always focus *all* of my attention on a beautiful woman," I said kissing her lightly on her plush lips.

"Unacceptable," she said running her delicate fingers up and down my exposed shaft. "Now you have to be punished for your actions. Since you didn't give me all of your attention, you'll have to give me all of you."

The mushroom head of my dick swelled so big, so tight, I thought I was going to burst when she leaned down and began suckling my balls. It was difficult controlling myself with *Trey Songs* in the background, telling me to dive in. The rhythm of her tongue and the music created a wild sensation throughout my body. I gently maneuvered her up until her mouth was angled along with the head of my erection. As soon as the song made it to the stroke part of the song, I caught my rhythm. I took long deep strokes in her wet dripping mouth. I picked up the remote from the coffee table, hitting repeat on the CD player. When I felt myself about to cum, I flipped Rubae' over, ripping the flimsy silk gown from her body.

After kissing my essence from her lips, I placed my hard member between her small luscious globes and aimed for the small O she made with her lips. Making contact, I forced her mouth open wider as I slid deeper down her throat. She grabbed my ass and pulled *me* deeper into her mouth with each stroke. By the time my first nut came, her face was already covered in saliva. She coughed and choked as I wouldn't release her head from the strong grip I held on her hair. Too paralyzed to move until every last drop was out.

Once my limbs was relaxed, I removed myself from her face and sat back on the sofa while she went into the bathroom. Not even a minute passed when she was back with a towel in her hands wiping her face.

"I hope you're not tired," she said removing her small traveling bag from beside the sofa. The zipper was open just enough, where I could see all kinds of sex toys and gels. "Your punishment isn't over, yet."

Chapter 8

Ella D............

Look at how this ungrateful bitch been livin. She should be happy I gave birth to her ass. It's been plenty of times I thought about shoving a wire hanger up my pussy. I know she knows me. Pat Ann wouldn't leave this earth without telling her who gave birth to her. That damn boy Tatum, paid everybody in Houma to say they didn't know who her mother was. May Belle's country ass can't even spell Mercedes, and that's if she can pronounce it.

But that's okay. These uppity people came looking for me anyway. Hate they found me in Vegas on the pole though. But they found me none-the-less. Bozy just want me to think they brought us here under false pretenses. Truth is, I don't care why we here. She's my daughter, so I deserve to live in the lap of luxury, too. Stingy bitch can't have it all. She probably would've been a little nicer if Bozy hadn't attacked her with those damn snakes.

"There you are."

Motif's sexy ass. His son looks like a God, but he's married to my daughter.

Can't touch that.

But I can flirt with the former Chief, even though he's married, too. But I'm accepting to powerful men who think they life is over because they no longer have that power anymore.

Damn. The painful look on his face when them Council people announced his son and new daughter-in-law, *Mr. and Mrs. Tatum De'amadre; Chief and Mistress of Gerillian Island,* must've hit him right in the gut. Dude looked like he was about to drop some tears.

"Nice to see you again……," I didn't know what to call him. I couldn't call him 'Pitiful sad man.' Shit naw, he got money.

"Please call me Motif," he said, already reaching for my hand before he came to a complete stop inches in front of me.

Unlike his older son, who could easily be mistaken for the beautiful God *Adonis* himself, Motif looked like a leering pervert who was hit with the beauty stick. His nails were well manicured. Probably never done a day's work in his life. His upper body was losing some of its muscle tone and his legs looked like they belong on a mannequin. This man spent a lot of time being pampered. I guess being filthy fucking rich does that to you.

"Have you had lunch, yet," he said, licking his thin lips.

Not someone I would want to kiss every night, but fuck it. Money is money.

"Actually, I'm in the mood for ice cream," I said, holding tight to his hand. "Sucking and licking has always been my favorite part of a meal."

His wide smile disappeared, when someone behind me caught his attention. I turned just as Bozy walked up to us.

"How are you again, Motif? Do you mind if I have a word with El alone?"

"Of course. Until later, Ms. Beau," he said with a small bow of his head and a wink of an eye.

After Motif walked away, Bozy started in on the bullshit. "Always on the job, huh El?"

"What the fuck is wrong with you? All these hoe's on this island and you can't find no one to chase, but me. Can't you just be happy I gave birth to the brat and it finally paid off," I said walking back to the courtyard.

"Dammit El, would you please stop and think for a minute. Or is that a concept you still haven't mastered, yet. These people came looking for us years later, after they were told we were dead."

"That was all Merry's doing. Ungrateful brat was willing for us to miss her wedding. If it wasn't for Motif and his staff searching for us to share in the special occasion, we would've never knew about the big nest egg she's sittin on."

Shaking his head at me, Bozy said, "Do you believe half the shit that pops up in your head? Bitch, you never even popped a tit in the girl's mouth. Why the fuck would she invite us to her wedding, when we didn't lift a finger to do shit for her, her entire life?" He thought a moment. "Fuck this. I'm wasting my time talking to you." He turned to leave. "Oh," he said, turning back. "One other thing. While you're sucking Motif off, use that time to think about the fact that your daughter is the Mistress of an entire island and her new husband just took leadership of everybody on this island from the man you're about to fuck. So whatever you do, you better not let him fuck her over or I'll finally have my reason to fuck you up."

I watched him until he walked back into the palace.

Fuck him.

Because he's beautiful, doesn't mean he's smart. Boy, Bozy really knows how to fuck up a day. For all he know, Motif probably just want some pussy like every straight man on this earth. And as far as Jameria goes, that bitch could give a flying fuck how and with who I spend my time. If it's left up to her, I'll be off this island before she get back from her honeymoon. But from the looks of what she's banging, I wouldn't be surprised if her stay was extended.

Dammit! I let Bozy get in my head.

I have to admit, Merry turned out to be a real beauty, though. Hate that she received Bozy's curse, but it was inevitable. Hours after I gave birth, snakes was lined up on Pat Ann's doorstep. Scared the shit out of me. A couple of days later, I found Bozy and told him what happened. I didn't even give him time to respond. I just told him to get that kid away from my mama before that brat kill her. I hopped on some shithead's bike and got the hell out of there.

I told Pat Ann she was a fool for keeping that baby. The last thing she said to me before I left was that the kid might turn out ten times better than me now that I won't be around to mess her up. Well, the joke's on her, because that kid was messed up the day she was conceived.

Every time I called her to get a piece of change, her excuse was always, she had to save for Merry. Not long after that, she had her number changed and unlisted. When I finally tracked Bozy down, who was still living in Louisiana, he told me when he went to get the kid Pat Ann all but slammed the door in his face.

Damn, he's such an idiot.

Now he wants to play 'Super Dad,' and find every conspiracy around the corner. What he need to be doing is finding some rich bitch to fall in. What did he do to me? Bozy got my head so cloudy, I can't think straight. I went back to the south wing of the palace where the guest are housed. As soon as I opened my door, I saw an envelope on the floor addressed to me. I picked it up and headed straight for the bathroom to the large claw foot tub to run my bath.

Going back to the sitting room, I retrieved a Newport from my purse, a douche from my suitcase and went to the toilet with Motif's letter to take a dump. After cleansing my sugar shack thoroughly, I lite my cigarette, taking a drag, while reading the letter.

Dear Ella,

It seems every time our paths cross, the time we spend together is short lived and the distractions is a constant for a man in my position. As in-laws, I think it would be in our best interest to socialize and get to know each other, as we are now family. Please join me for dinner tonight in my private chambers at 8. I will send my guard to escort you. I so look forward to your company.

Until then,

Motif

Well, well, well. It seems former Chief Motif is interested, after all. This is cause for a special outfit. Motif told me the yacht would be available to me whenever I needed it and as long as I'm on this island, I didn't have to worry about money. All I had to do was drop his name. Come to think of it, I knew a couple of pimps like that who thought they could put me on a stroll......

After taking a leisurely bath, I tossed on my floral sarong and yellow sandals. Grabbing my wide brim floppy hat and knock off shades, I left the palace and headed straight for the docks. Just as the guard escorted me on the boat, to take me to the mainland, I saw Noonie hurrying from the courtyard.

"Do you mind if I join you? It's been so long since I've been shopping with another female," she said already climbing aboard.

"Not at all. I was just headed out to purchase an outfit for dinner and to get my hair and nails done." No need to tell her I'm getting all gussied up for her husband.

"Great. I'm glad to accompany you. I can take you to my hairstylist." After a beat passed, she asked, "Would you care for a glass of wine as we journey?"

"Thank you," I said, taking the flute. "You mention that you don't go on female outings......I'm surprise to hear you haven't went on many shopping sprees with my daughter."

"Oh yes," she said with a slight smile. "Don't get me wrong, I'm quite sure if Jameria and I had met on different terms, we would've had that mother daughter relationship like I wanted, but I guess it just wasn't in the cards for us, either."

"I don't understand," I said. Bozy's theories playing havoc in my head.

"Oh......I thought you knew since you're family and all. It was Tatum who found Jameria, but his uncle Demarcus adopted her. They wouldn't let no one get within ten feet of her, unless you were a part of their pack."

Now I get it. Merry was royalty even before her marriage to the former Chief's son."But I'm not complaining," she continued. "I understand they have to keep her close. As Mistress of Geri Island, her schooling and training is the upmost important thing in her life. But as a mother and friend, I think being young is important, too. But how can you, when so many people looks up to you?

"Whenever she step into the palace gardens, the people greet her as if she is a fallen angel. And the children adores her. Every Tuesdays and Thursdays she's either tutoring or visiting one of her many charity organizations. Her and the pack girls even took me to Bali for my birthday a couple of years ago.....I just hate the way things ended between us."

Well, I guess this is the part where I take the bait. "What happened," I asked all concerned.

She hesitated for a moment, like she was bothered. "Well, I shouldn't be saying this, but a few months back, Tatum and Jameria were going through some things. Tatum came to me for some advice and support. One thing lead to another, the next thing I know, I'm pregnant.

"I went to Tatum about my condition, telling him I wanted to have an abortion. But he refused and started talking nonsense about his first born son and how delighted he was becoming a father. That was until Jameria burst through the door......God, I was so glad when I regained consciousness, but upset I had lost the baby after what Jameria did to me," she said with tears streaming down her uplifted face.

"If Tatum wanted the baby so bad, why didn't he defend you," I said with just enough sympathy in my voice and a soft hand on her shoulder to make her think I really give a shit.

"Tatum is just as afraid of Jameria as the rest of the Pack. If it wasn't for Demarcus, Tatum probably would've sent her home months ago. But it could also have been the fact that Tatum wanted to become Chief at such a young age. I mean he could've waited until he was twenty-one. What's a couple of years?"

This bitch is slow.

Do she really think I believe a man looking like him would even waste his time glancing at her? I don't even think he would touch her with a stick. Hell, I'm having trouble looking at her my-damn-self. She just don't know though, I'm on to her shit. She's from an island, but I'm from the dirty, dirty.

I decided to play her little game, anyway. "You'll have to excuse me Noonie, for digging so deep into your personal life. Hopefully the situation can be resolved since we are all family now."

Obviously this fool didn't know Jameria was already pregnant when she walked down the aisle. Though, I know that boy,

Tatum is beyond crazy about her, it's still a shot gun wedding anyway you look at it. Like this dummy in front of me said, 'What's a couple of years?' A two year old heir, you dumb bitch, that's what.

But really? The boy leaving Merry, for her?

Bitch, please!

Merry and Noonie is like strawberries and onions. Ain't no way in hell this bitch is going to get me to believe, sexy, god looking Tatum, ever rolled around between the sheets with her.

Nope. Just can't make me believe it.

Chapter 9

Noonie.......

Motif's trying to cut me out of the deal, since I got pregnant with Boaz's baby........if I gave him the right condom, that is. It still didn't matter in the end.

It was months ago, when I took Motif up on his offer to let the two youngest members of the new leading Pack to run a train on me. Those boys fucked me three-ways-from-Sunday. Pierce worked me with ten inches while Boaz pound me with twelve. By the time they got through with my pussy AND ass, I was raw. They both came in me so many times, I lost count. Hell, I only gave them one condom a piece.

Who knew teens fucked like beasts?

I won't lie, as soon as I felt the head of Pierce's dick enter my asshole, I thought I was a goner, until I felt Boaz's erection enter my vaginal walls, seconds later. They both seesawed in me vigorously until I felt like I was being tortured. But the horror of the whole thing was that, it was Pierce who came in me more times than Boaz. Sometimes, I wasn't even wet when he came.

I would've been on my knees, thanking Jameria for killing the unknown bastard child, if Motif hadn't woken from his coma saying everything was my damn fault. I should've had guards outside of Tatum's door waiting on that bitch before she came in the room. Instead, Tatum recognized it was me before I got the dick out the drawers and Jameria bust in, beating my ass into silent dreams. And after all that shit I went through, the only thing Motif can say to me is, "your fault."

But Motif is going to get his.

He didn't have to be the grieving husband. Sending me some flowers would have showed he cared a little bit. But all I get is crap all the time. And what the fuck did he mean, 'this is the last time?' Like he's going to get rid of me or something. Well, I'm not going to sit around here and wait for that shit to happen. I'm going to wait for the test results to come back and present them to Council. Even if I didn't get Tatum, at least I can take Motif's second born down with me. And since Jameria's biological parents is new to this land, they're open to any game. I already got the backwoods mother on board. All I have to do, is get the beautiful, fucked-up father on my side ant the game will change in my favor.

Now all I have to do is wear the perfect outfit for my man trap. Thanks to Jameria, I'll have to work harder, since I won't be giving up the pussy tonight. But at least I can get him off twice, using hands and mouth. No man on this island can resist my blowjob action. Well, except for Tatum and most of his pack brothers. The young ones were easy to fool. But the rest look at me with disgust as if I was beneath them.

Well, fuck them all!!!!

Once I get the other snake charmer on my side, the whole lot of them will be kissing my ass. Especially Motif, since he decided to fuck me over with this baby bullshit.

"Wow, this is beautiful," the country bumkin next to me was saying.

"Take it. It's on me." Is she seriously planning on wearing that? Pink skirt, plaid top, and cream pumps. Where the fuck is she going? To a classic circus rodeo. "Hot date tonight?"

"The hottest," she said modeling her ridiculous outfit in the mirror.

I was surprised when I laid eyes on Jameria's mother. When she first arrived, I thought they pick up the wrong person. This plan Jane woman cannot be Jameria's mother. Until I saw the small feathers in her peaches and cream face. And regardless of her culture being Caucasian, you can actually *smell* the Sioux linage in her blood. Her scent is a fresh woodsy fragrance, covered up by heavy cologne. Nothing like Jameria's natural berry scent. Her scent is so strong, you'd swear she bathe in blackberries and strawberries all day.

The scent of a woman is something Shyamae' taught me.

Surprised the shit out of me when she got between my legs for inspection, before licking. She didn't waste any time introducing my ass to *Summer's Eve* either. 'Your natural odor is whack. Sorry there won't be any dining, until you get your diet and estrogen level tight.' She and Boaz showed up at my suite one night unannounced, claiming to be his future mate, but immediately let me know she was on my side, as long as I help her become Mistress of Geri Island......and Boaz was all for it.

It seems the girl Jameria found for Boaz was a wrecking ball waiting to happen. And when she told me her gift, I was on board. As long as she had the right training, I'd follow her to the end of time and back. The girl can eat pussy so good, she had me calling her *my* queen.

But Shy is not the issue.

My problem is Boaz.

He knows he have me cornered. Fuck his age. The boy is pure evil on two long muscled legs. He wasn't no Tatum, who resembled the god *Apollo*, but he could defiantly hold his own. He left no doubt in my mind that if he go down, he was taking a few people with him. Especially when he found out I was pregnant. I told him the baby was needed if he still planned on being Chief of Geri. By him and Tatum sharing the same gene pool, it would've been my word against Tatum's, since Motif had a vasectomy and Boaz so young in age. It wouldn't have worked no way since I found out Motif is not Tatum's father. But all that shit aside, I still need to get to Boaz, before he gets to me. Then there's the other thing.

Something is going on. Something big. And Tatum, Jameria, and Demarcus knows what it is. It is something so big, that during the boys' last hunt, Jameria and Demarcus would have these private discussions over dinner. I could never hear what they were saying, but every now and then, they would take out a map. And since I woke from my coma, Demarcus handsome face was starting to show worry lines across his smooth forehead.

 On our way back to the island, I asked Ella if she wanted to get together for dinner later, hopefully to give me some insight on her plans.

"Well actually, I have a date. How about we meet for lunch tomorrow?"

Okay. She eased out of that one smoothly. "I have a lunch meeting. You know, the wife of a Chief is always busy. Want to meet for breakfast?"

"Late sleeper. Not really a morning person. But I tell you what, how about we meet at that waterfall that's so popular on your island. I heard one of your elders speak of how majestic it looks from sunset to nightfall. I hear your people visit it daily for hours."

"Oh yes. The Blue Mist," I said smiling to myself. But what she don't know is the attraction wasn't the waterfall, but Tatum and his entire pack training in practically nothing. Their bare chests glistening in the sun, as they man handled their mates. Using their bodies as weapons, tossing and grabbing limbs high in the air, as the females showed off their acrobatic skills of combat. The young Pack made the art of war seem like a sensual dance for lovers. "Of course. How about we meet tomorrow evening around five?"

"Not a problem," she said leaving the dock in a hurry, as soon as Motif came into view.

Yeah. She's got a date alright.

I hope he take her country ass to the finest restaurant and the best shops in Brazil. In her case, she'll probably choose to go to the palace bathroom, thinking it's a tourist attraction. But I hope she knows the heavy price she'll have to pay fucking with someone like Motif. When the time comes for him to fall, hopefully she's smart enough to move out of the way. And he's going to fall hard. Because, if I don't get him, Tatum and Jameria will.

Chapter 10

Bozy...........

"Glad I finally caught you in your quarters. Sorry we weren't able to meet sooner." I stood there staring at a woman who was probably beautiful.....or not. I couldn't tell.

Look like she had some Botox work done, but certain areas in her face (especially the forehead) had yellowish marks all over it, as if she was in a fight for her life. Her eyes were sunken with dark circles around them and her entire face was swollen. But her body was all manufactured. She had fake toenails, fake fingernails, bun implants, breast implants, and because of the short purple top barely covering her belly button, I could distinctively see the marks from her tummy tuck.

What the fuck is this standing in front of me?

"Hello, I'm Noonie. Chief Motif's mate."

So this Motif's so called 'beautiful mate,' as he described her. I think he left out a few details. But really, this is the woman Motif said ran the island as Mistress, until my daughter was the proper age.........or at least that's what Motif's claiming.

It didn't take me long after mingling with the people of this island, to learn that Jameria practically ran this place with an iron fist from the moment she stepped off the boat at age thirteen. And it was also obvious to me that Noonie's respect level in the community was so low, it had me wondering if she led the life of a *puta* in her younger days.

I extended my hand to her. "Nice to meet you. What can I do for you this evening," I said, firmly retrieving my hand from her grip.

My phone in my quarters started ringing.

"Excuse me," I said, leaving the deformed woman standing in my sitting room doorway. "Hello?"

"Bozy it's me, El. I was on my way to your room when I saw ole girl headed to your door. Get rid of her. We need to talk. It seems you were right. These uppity mothafucka's is messing with the wrong bitch if they think I'm gone let them do sumthin' to my kin. I'll fuck all these bitches up. They don't know who they fuckin' wit, she said. Her Cajun tongue trying to force its way out in anger.

Not sure if the Noonie monster could speak any other languages. I went for broke and addressed El in our Cajun tongue. *"Sa fe` ou chaje lide ou?"* (What made you change your mind?)

"Oh god!! Not that tongue again. Anyway, let's just say former Chief Motif would do anything to get his title back........including taking out his own son. Stop speaking gibberish and get your ass over here.

"Give me a few minutes," I said before hanging up.

Taking a deep breath, I faced the deformed woman, ready to deliver my lie, but she was not there. Several articles of clothing were present though. All leading to my bedroom. Right there, on the doorknob, a lace bra was hanging from it.

I didn't even bother to finish the hunt.

If El can admit I was right about *one* thing, then that's a historical moment. But if something is causing her to have to defend someone other than herself, then it had to be hell to pay.

I hurriedly left my suite and whatever else that's in it and headed for El's room.

Before I made it to her door, her signature scent *'Gio,'* hit me hard. It was the first thing that drew me to her. But the attraction didn't last long. There was no way my people would let me live, if Ella had stayed with me.

And being white had nothing to do with it.

Ella D was in another man's face before my seed even hit the egg.

When she heard my father had no money and was rich in land only, she read me my rights of being another broke ass black man. What she didn't know was my great-great-great-grandfather was full Hopi Indian who own slaves in the south and passed a hundred acres off to his first born son, who was also a slave. The hundred acres have been passed down from generation to generation. The same hundred aces I plan to leave to my one and only daughter that I cannot deny is mine.

As soon as I found out what El said about Jameria was true, I went to my grandfather for the truth. I'd been told since birth that it was impossible for me to have kids with only one testicle, plus I also have the rare gift of snake charming. Like her honey eyes, snake charming is another trait we also share. My grandfather told me to put El aside and take care of my child. "'If the people of this small town is talking then you need to listen. Teach the last heir of your great-great-great-grandfather's blood, the art of snake charming. That gift has skipped several generations, not knowing if any of us will ever see that rarity again. We've always thought that it would leave this world forever the day you pass on. Jameria belongs with her people for the proper training. You need to get her and bring her to her people.'"

It took me years just to get close enough to see the beautiful black child who played with snakes. Her grandmother nor the snakes would let

me get within twenty feet of the child. Hanging from trees and hiding in shadows only made the snakes she possessed, more fidgety. But I wanted to see her. I just couldn't stay away. I was so desperate to get my daughter back, that I asked a couple of friends to help me out. A few suffered because of me.

Poor Kevin.

His plan was to go to Ms. Pat Ann claiming he was ill from a minor cold, then he was going to run and snatch the child. I told him it was stupid before he got the last words out. But what can I say.....young people do stupid things. As a surprise and true honor of friendship, Kevin decided to follow through with his plan. By the time I got his note and figured out what he was going to do, I was almost too late. A huge fucking rock python had already broken four of his ribs and pretty little Jameria had just skipped around the post in the road back to her grandmother's house.

Even then she was too strong for her age.

I had to watch my daughter grow up from a distance. Always anxious to hear when Ms. Pat Ann was in town, just to have one of my own snakes get me a good hiding spot close to the house to watch her play and to make sure she was safe. Then one day I walked into May Sue's Place where May Belle was telling the locals about the group of young men who came looking for the girl. After that I never heard anything else or seen the child again. I tried to coax information from May Belle, but it was obvious that she was getting paid pretty good to keep her mouth shut.

Then after many years and prayers later, they were finally answered when this huge Indian walked up behind me like *I* surprised *him*. But it was his features that really had me amazed.

In this day and age not too many natives wear their hair long anymore. This man's hair was parted in the middle with two thick long braids that came to his tapered waist. We stood there staring at each other. My mind on the wrench lying on the hood of the car I'd been working on. If this big motherfucker came here for business then he needed to speak his case. Anything else is a guaranteed ass whippin.

Then he said, as if to himself, "'The resemblance is remarkable.'"

And from that phrase alone, I knew the man was there about my daughter.

El opened the door after the first knock. "Come on in, Bozy. I tried to take a quick shower while you got rid of the Botox queen."

"I didn't get rid of her. Just left her in there and came straight here. Didn't want to find out why all of her clothes were on the floor."

"Are you serious? She's in your room naked? Where did you tell her you were going," she said looking down the hall, before she closed the door locking it.

"I didn't tell her shit. I'm guessing she's in my bedroom waiting for me to make an appearance. But I decided if I want to keep my lunch down, it was best that I left the room as quickly as possible." That got her laughing. I'd forgotten her melodious laugh. "Besides, nothing is going to make me miss the monumental moment. Did I not hear you correctly on the phone when you said I was right about something," I said, walking further in the room. She had her long bleach blond hair pulled into a ponytail. Her light blue eyes dropping to the thick carpet beneath her bare feet as she crossed her slender arms over the silky oriental robe that barely covered

her backside. I could tell she was having trouble admitting she was wrong, but it will be a cold day in hell before I make it easy on her.

"Bozy, we have to get Merry off of this island. I have no idea what Pat Ann was thinking, but these people mean her no good." She looked at me then. I could see the fear and anger in her eyes. "Bozy," she pleaded, tears streaming down her peaches and cream cheeks. "He wants her dead, Bozy. He wanted her dead years ago," she said, falling into the beige leather high back chair. "The fool actually thought I hated my own child so much, I would want to help him plan her murder."

I knew from the moment I met the man, he was dangerous. At first I thought the big native that came to my shake was the man himself. Instead he'd sent his six bodyguards to retrieve me, telling me some bullshit about my presence was needed due to the affect my daughter was having on this island. But once Chief Motif eyes landed on my chocolate skin, the introduction was over before it began.

"I told you that guy was full of shit. Tell me what happened," I said taking a seat on the long leather couch.

She propped her bare feet up on the coffee table, sinking further down on the plush cushion. The short robe showing more of those luscious thighs I never had a chance to memorize. "He invited me to dinner in his chambers. And believe me when I tell say his room is worth more than everything on this island. The man has gold trim plates with diamonds in the glass. Anyway, he started off with the dumb bullshit, saying he was surprised that Jameria could be a daughter of mine, 'You would think *two* African-Americans were her biological parents," she mimicked.

I had to laugh at that one myself. A paternity test was not needed in our case. The African-American beauty looked as if she had none of her Caucasian linage. It was more like a *maternity* test should've been given instead. Jameria looked as if she was cloned from my grandma, herself.

"I thought you said the girl was evil walking on two legs. What made you start caring now?"

El looked at me like I'd lost my damn mind. "I don't give a damn if the girl created hell herself. The point is *no one*, and I do mean *no one* fucks with one of our own. Our Cajun blood runs deep in that girls' veins and as long as I'm around that blood will not be spilled. It hurts me to my heart that I'm about to become a grandmother at such a young age, but I'll be damn if I let a bitch like Motif fuck with her over some dirt."

I was shocked by everything she just said. "What the fuck is you talking about? Grandmother? What aren't you telling me El?"

She let out an exasperated breath. "Please tell me you are not dumb to the fact that Merry is pregnant?"

"Jameria's pregnant," was the only two words I could utter.

"Oh give it a rest Bozz. That girl is more than capable enough to raise a child. Hell, she's been leader of this country for years. If she can make an island prosper, she can raise a kid."

And she says *I'm* dumb to the fact. "El do you remember your pregnancy?"

"Of course I do. It was the worst experience of my- Oh. My God!"

I knew that brain of hers would finally catch up.

El jumped up out of her chair and ran straight for her closet to retrieve her luggage. "I gotta get the hell out of here! This place is a fucking snake pit," she said, throwing whatever she got her hands on in the suitcase.

"Calm down El. As long as Jameria is not on the island the snakes are at bay. We're safe.....for now. Look let's get out of here and go take a look at that waterfall everybody's talking about, I said soothingly."

She eased away from the suitcases, but continued to rummage through her garments until she settled on a lime green, form fitting, running outfit. "God, Bozy. What has that girl gotten herself into," she said letting her short robe drop to the floor.

Still the same ole El. Never afraid to show the world exactly who she is.

"I don't know, but when she gets back, we're going to have to talk to her and she'll have no choice but to listen."

"Are you serious? I abandoned her as a child and you challenged her at her own wedding. She's not going to listen to a damn thing we have to say."

She was right. I had no idea what the hell came over me to do that to my own child. And there's no way I'm going to ask her new husband for help.........or any of the so called, 'Wolf Pack.' The entire group looked half-crazed when it came to their Mistress. To get within a foot of her would be impossible. And I don't know why, but it's something about that boy Tatum that reminds me of someone. I can't remember who, but the boy's entire aura screams danger. No I cannot go to him for help.

"What about her step-father?"

"What about him," I said looking up in time as she laid her hairbrush down and pulled her green top down over her breast.

"Maybe we can talk to him. Tell him what former Chief Motif have planned for his daughter."

Damn. Those words stung.

"Sorry, Bozz," she said taking a deep breath, flopping down next to me. "Didn't mean it the way I said it."

"It's cool, El. I get it. From my own observation at the wedding reception, I could tell that Jameria is very close to her adopted father. You're right. If we're going to help her, the only way to do that is through the young Elder Demarcus."

We both sought there for a while lost in our own thoughts when we heard a knock at the sitting room door.

"I wonder who that could be. I didn't order room service or anything." Ella D. peeped out of the door hole. Her lips curved into a smile as she motioned for me to join her at the door.

As soon as I peeped out of the tiny hole, I wished I hadn't. The deformed woman named Noonie was standing on the other side about to knock again.

"Hello? Ella? Are you in there?"

I quickly put my hand over El's mouth when she was about to answer. Then we heard a key being inserted into the lock.

I grabbed her arm and pulled her into the coat closet.

"Hello? Ella?"

We watched through the bi-folds of the door as the woman went through El's closets, drawers, and nightstands. She was about to enter our hiding spot when one of the snakes I'd brought with me, slithered pass Noonie's feet under the couch. She tripped over the side table, knocking her and the priceless lamp on the shiny marble floor. Shattering the lamp and pissing her pants during the collision. She jumped up running out of the room, slamming the door behind her.

"Dammit Bozy! Why did you put a snake in my room? Could you please put those things in a cage before someone gets hurt?"

"I didn't. They go where they're needed. One of them probably followed me or been in here for days. Anyway, that Noonie is kind of crazy. I wonder what she's after."

"Well, trust me when I say, it's not her husband. That chick is a freak. My eyes might've been playing tricks on me, but I think the woman got it bad for her oldest son. Did you see how she was staring at that Tatum? Like it was five o' clock meal time and he was the main course."

Damn. I guess El isn't as slow as I thought her to be. "Yeah. I saw that too. The woman was literally salving from her mouth."

El walked out of her closet and took her cell out of her pocket. "That boy who was part of the wedding party slipped me a number. I think he said his name was Pierce."

"Why would he give you his number when it's obvious his loyalty lies with Jameria? They have every right not to trust us, but he gave you his number?"

"You said it yourself Bozy. We were lead here under false pretense and that boy knows something. He slid it in my hand during your confrontation with our daughter, you ass. Anyway, when I looked at him confused, the only thing he said was, 'you'll know when to use it.' So I figured with a freaky deformed bitch going through my shit and a jackass with limited power set on destroying one of my own, is reason enough for me to use this number. Maybe he can help us get in touch with that Demarcus guy."

Chapter 11

Motif.........

"I want them dead! Tatum and that bitch Jameria should've been dead years ago."

Remy. My right hand man. One of the three members left from my 'Wolf Pack.' Two were found dead and one has been missing for two years now. "We're trying Motif, but please understand we're at a disadvantage. Tatum's woman is a real *"Luandinha."* We were so desperate, we hired professional assassins to take them out, but for some reason the assassins are the ones being taken out."

Fuck!

Tatum has been a thorn in my side since the day his punk ass took his first breath. I should've killed him years ago when I had the chance. As soon as I found out the little shit wasn't my seed, I should've flushed his ass down the toilet.

"What about that *chicka*, El," Remy asked, bringing me back to the regretted present.

I looked at him. Ready to snap on his ass for addressing me with a question. Then I had to remember that I'm no longer chief of a priceless island, no longer leader of his people, no longer king of unfound treasures. Just a wealthy common man now. So I just responded to the fucking question.

"What about her?"

Remy's a six foot five inch muscle bound native from my island. My first choice as my right hand. He didn't fear me, but the concern look that was visible in his yellow-green eyes, quickly dissipated after my response. "Do you think she'll help us? I know what you said about her being money hungry. Maybe if we offer her a small fortune....."

I was already shaking my head. "Not going to work. I'd offered her something far greater than a little piece of change. I invited the bitch to dinner and presented her with a whole new life. But as soon as I started talking about getting rid of the new leading couple, her fist and lips was in battle of with which could pull the tightest."

I couldn't believe how my date ended. Actually it ended before it really began. Ella D. Beau was not what I expected as Jameria's mother. When I first found out she didn't even want the girl, I wasted no time contacting her. But after one dinner date, I knew I should've left her ass stripping.

"What about the father? Wait. On second thought, never mind."

"Why never mind," I asked.

"Call me crazy, but the man was staring at your son like a long-lost-lover or something. The odd thing was, he was staring at Tatum and not Jameria."

Remy's words mirrored my thoughts. The second I met Bosuer I knew I'd made a terrible mistake bringing him here. Unlike Ella D. who'd shown no interest in the girl (at first), the man they call Bozy feelings for Jameria spoke loud and clear in his eyes at the mere mention of her name, until he laid eyes on Tatum. The man couldn't keep his eyes off the boy.

"Neither of them is of good use," I said sighing. "Well, Tatum isn't twenty-one yet, so I still have a chance to reclaim my position as chief until Boaz turns eighteen." My true son.

"Umm.....I don't think.......Have you heard....." Remy kept looking from me to the door like he wanted to run for his life.

"Just spit it out, man!"

He jumped like I'd shocked him with a Taser. "There's a rumor going around that the Mistress is pregnant."

Once the words left his mouth, everything in my eye sight was red. Before I realize what I was doing, I attack poor Remy, sending blow after blow into his smooth tan face, which was now swelling and streaming with blood. He didn't even try to fight back. Such a loyal servant.

My hand became numb with pain from the first blow, plus I was exhausted within seconds of the attack. Tatum and his bitch made me look like a fool. People who use to fear me now laugh in my face or whisper as I pass. There was no way my surviving pack members is going to see me as some bitch who can't last *two minutes* in a one way fight. After a minute and a few seconds later, I stood taking deep breaths, not even offering the man a hand up. He stood breathing evenly with a swollen eye, a blooded nose (that probably wasn't even broken) and a busted lip, like nothing ever happened.

"It was just a rumor, Motif. Don't you think if Council had got wind of it, you would've known by now?"

Has he forgotten that I'm no longer chief. Hell, I'm not even an elder. "They don't have to tell me shit! Fuck Council. Boaz would have told me if Jameria was pregnant or not."

Remy looked at me like I am the biggest dummy in the world. "Motif, I've known you all of our lives and we have seen and done a lot of shit together. We have agreed and bumped heads many times, and whether it was right or wrong, I'd follow your lead with my head held high, walking proud behind you. But on this one, I'm hoping you would use a little common sense and see that Boaz love his brother. He's a part of his pack. Like me, he would die for his Chief. Loyalty is partof a man's strength, and it radiates from Boaz body like a second skin. When it comes to Jameria and Tatum, even though you want to believe otherwise, the boy sees love AND hate. A struggle in all teenagers' life. What makes you think he would betray the two people he's struggling over?"

How could I tell him the truth? That Tatum is his half-brother. Spit from the same womb, but not planted by the same seed. If I had the chance, I'd kill that bitch again.

Ky.

That fucking *punta*, betrayed me many times over. But giving birth to that bastard was my undoing. But the bitch lived. Even after a deep penetration on my part, still the brat slid out like water. When the bitch passed out for those few minutes, I wanted to strangle her. End her life right then and there, (even before I found out he wasn't my son), but she came to, and there was nothing I could do in a room full of people. And to make matters worse, Vilmander, her father, knew the entire time the kid wasn't mine. Blackmail was the only way for me to keep my title. A legacy I planned to pass to my REAL son."Don't worry about Boaz. He won't disappoint me," I said to the man's skeptical face.

"Forgive me Motif. I meant no disrespect toward neither of your sons. But, I just don't want this to be a scandal as big as the one fifteen years ago...."

If I wasn't exhausted, I'd get up and beat his ass again. "If you value your life, never bring that up again. Go find Noonie. I sent her to go check out Ella D. and she hasn't come back yet." Just as he was leaving, my three o' clock appointment sashayed through the door. Before Remy got too far out, I yelled, "On second thought, fuck Noonie. When she has some information for me to redeem herself, she knows where to find me. Close of the doors to the wing and come back here. I owe you for spilling your blood.

My three o' clock had sashayed into my sleeping chambers, removing her clothes as she completed her journey. I may have lost my crown, but I still have my pussy privilege. What I once thought was gained by power, proven to be false. I earned those privileges by dick and mouth.

It amazed me how many aging elders married pussy young enough to be their granddaughters. As soon as I made it to this island, pussy was coming to me before anyone knew I was here to be trained as Chief. I've fucked leading ladies, diplomats' wives, foreign leaders' wives, and even my father-in-law's second wife. I fucked so many women in one day, I started taking those damn blue pills to keep my dick hard, plus I had to put the bitches on a schedule.

Like right now, my three o' clock is the wife of the elder who made my life a living hell.

Elder Nuieve.

The only person I hate more than Tatum. The late Vilmander's best-friend who was also his trusted right-hand man to the late Chief's Wolf Pack. I should've killed his ass when I took out Vilmander. But I needed the leverage.

Keeping Nuieve alive was a must. He was valuable to my reign as Chief, until the shit decided to go behind my back and suggested to Council to let Tatum train as Chief at an early age. I would normally get the information from his wife who's now on her knees sucking my pole. Kilmya is Nuieve's 29 year old wife. They married when she was twenty-two and he was fifty-six. But, did he seriously think that he could handle this freak? So for his lacking in the sex department, I thrived over the tell-tale stories his bitch was moaning to me as I waxed her pussy. But it was obvious he didn't tell her everything. Especially Tatum's little come-up.

Remy returned with a fresh clean face and a partially swollen eye. He watched Kilmya as she swallowed the last of my seed. He then looked at me, holding his long hard bulge through his pants. I gave a nod and he came forward, grabbing her by her long thick hair, pulling her mouth off dick and shoving his down her throat. I went into the bathroom, while Remy hammered his dick in the girls' mouth. Listening to her gags, I downed two blue pills with a cup of water, jacking myself, so I could rejoin the party. It took a while, but I manage to get myself firm enough before I decided to let her do the rest. By the time I made it back to the bedroom, Remy had the girl in the missionary position, with her legs wrapped around the back of her neck.

In all the years I fucked Kilmya, never had she had the look of pure ecstasy on her face as she did now. She was practically begging for his pipe.

"Yes! Fuck me harder! Shove that big ass dick in my sloppy pussy....Yes!

Fuck! Me! Daddy," she kept repeating.

Damn! Bitch never did that when I was fucking her.

Remy was pounding his entire length in her like a sledgehammer. They'd finally noticed my presence when he lifted her to change positions. He lifted her completely off the bed and I took her place in the middle, lying flat on my back with my semi-hard erection laying on my stomach. Remy placed her back on the bed on her hands and knees. She crawled over my legs, angling her full red lips over my johnson while Remy made arrangements with her rear.

My thighs trembled from several little licks and kisses she gave my engorged member.

At the other end of the bed, I saw Remy dribble spit from his mouth onto her anus. With her own mouth full of my meat, her eyes rolled to the back of her head like she in heaven, when Remy plunged two thick fingers deep in her ass. She leaned forward, taking me to the back of her throat and giving my right-hand man full access to both holes.

While I was enjoying the best blowjob of my life, Noonie decided that was the time to make an entrance. She stared at me fuming with her hands on her hips like I actually give a shit.

"What is it," I asked. I had a firm grip on Kilmya's head, bringing her face down hard on my pole.

"I need to talk to you. Alone," she stressed.

Every day for the past fourteen years, I ask myself why I married this bitch. I have yet to come up with an answer.

I shoved Kilmya off my dick, showing my irritation as I climbed off the bed. As I followed her out the door, I got a good glimpse of Remy with his hand deep in Kilmya's ass. This might end up being a fun night if I don't let Noonie's bitch ass fuck it up for me.

"You know that's why people treat me like shit Motif. You have no respect for me at all. And what make matters worse, you got that bitch in there humming on your dick while I do all of your dirty work," she said, flopping her mangled ass down on my custom made ostrich skin couch.

"I don't want to hear that shit! Tell me what you found out, then get the fuck out. That way you won't see me disrespecting you."

"Fuck you, Motif! I ain't telling you shit! You always fucking over me, using my pussy as your own piggybank. Do you have any idea what I go through fucking that nasty ass Chief from the Keekelo tribe just to keep him from marrying off his ugly ass daughter? Which was a wasted effort anyway. All of your careful planning was worthless Motif! Tatum is married to Jameria. He never gave the Keekelo's daughter a second glance. I fucked that nasty mothafucka for nothing and you won't even say sorry."

"Noonie, I don't have shit to be sorry for. You is my bitch. When I tell you to do something, you do it with no questions asked. The same rules apply to YOU whether I'm Chief or not. Now I'm going to let your little outburst slide this time, but if you planning on it being a next time, bitch I'll kill you for even thinking you can talk to me like that. Now once again, what the fuck did you find out? And please make it quick. I want to get back to my appointment.

I stared at her once pretty face, before Jameria's attack made her a haggard bitter woman. Her face was so fucked-up, I couldn't tell if she was smiling or frowning. But at this particular moment, I could defiantly tell she was smiling.

"Jameria's pregnant," she said with obvious glee in her voice.

My pressure spiked to a whole new level. Noonie wiped the ugly look from her face before rushing to me.

"Motif are you alright," she said, guiding me to the sofa.

"This can't be happening," I said, clutching the arms of the over-stuffed chaise. This bitch was about to get the same beat down as Remy. I grabbed her by her arms. "How do you know?"

She pushed hard against my chest, almost falling on her ass removing herself from my grip. "What the fuck is wrong with you? I didn't knock her up. I'm just the messenger. Anyway," she said backing up several more paces away from me and closer to the door. "I went to that guy Bozy's suite to see if he wanted to join us for dinner tomorrow, but he wasn't in his rooms. I was on my way to that bitch Ella's room when I saw that servant you was fucking, coming from that way. I asked the hoe, what was the hurry and she said, the two of them was talking about going to the waterfall and she didn't want them to think she was eavesdropping. So I grabbed the bitch hand, like I was her friend or some shit and told her to follow me. I pulled her in the computer room with me and put my finger to my lips, indicating we should talk quietly. After a little coaxing she told me she heard Ella D. tell Bozy that the Mistress is pregnant. She said the woman knew the moment she set eyes on her daughter, even after eighteen years of non-communication. When I thought the coast was clear, I sent your fuck toy on her merry little way then I went to Ella's room to see what I could find out since she wasn't going to be there for a while. But the bitch had a snake guarding her shit, just like Jameria."

"What do you mean, just like Jameria? I thought her father was the snake charmer." From the little fiasco at the wedding reception, the woman Ella D. looked down right frighten of the things.

"I don't know, Motif. That dude Bozy, probably left it there. Here's the real question. What are you going to do about Jameria and her fetus? Tatum guards that girl like a fucking pit-bull and what he don't do, her snakes does the rest. I'm surprised Boaz didn't tell you."

Remy's words flashing like a bright light in my head.

"We're going to stick to the plan. Boaz *will* become Chief after me. Once Tatum and his pack of freaks get back, I'll go straight to Council, informing them of the continue failure of communication the royal couple insist on influencing the rest of their pack members to do. No respect for their elders," I said, trying to taper my anger down. "I can't believe Boaz did this to me."

"Boaz didn't do anything to you. The boy loves his brother. Maybe if you told him the truth about Tatum's parentage," she said smirking in my face. "Oh, that's right. You're afraid to tell your youngest son that your oldest son is fathered by their mother's true love of her life and that if anybody found out, you'll lose all rights with this island, including your legacy as Chief. Your home island will be known once again as the poorest land in the world."

I stared at the bitch. "And you'll lose your meal ticket. No expense accounts, no jewelry, no designer clothes, not even a royal pot to piss in. Your skank ass would have to return to the slums. And from the way Jameria fucked you up, it's going to be hard to get a John to look at you rather than fuck you." The bitch actually had the nerve to shed tears.

"Don't start crying now bitch. You brought that shit on yourself when you

tried to fuck Tatum."

"Everything I did Motif, I did for us," she said. Her ravaged face now drenched in tears.

"Bitch stop lying! You did that shit for yourself. Once you found out about Tatum'sparentage. You wasted no time trying to fuck him to have his first born."

"What other choice did I have," she screamed, pacing the room. "Every time you went after Jameria or Tatum the risks grew higher of you being expose. Don't you understand you became Chief under false pretense? Obviously you don't, because you're putting brother against brother with no explanation. The first born son of Ky is NOT YOUR SON. Do you remember Ky motherfucker? Huh? Do you? The true heir to this land. And you know as well as I do that Tatum is her true heir. The man who finally took his rightful place as Chief. A title that belonged to him the day his mother died." Her wild eyes bore holes in me as a sadistic laugh escaped from her lips. "For the past eighteen years you have be nothing but a thug acting as Chief.

"Like I said," slowly walking around her to my sitting room door. "The only person you tried to save was yourself. But you were a fool to think that Tatum is Captain Save-A-Hoe. Now get the fuck out of my chambers. I refuse to waste my energy on you when I got pussy in the next room."

She strolled to the door like she didn't have a care in the world. When she made it firmly over the threshold, she turned to say something, but I let the door slip from my fingers to close in her face. I didn't waste my time contemplating on what she said. Instead I made my way back to my bedroom to see Remy laying on his back and Kilmya with his dick rammed in her ass. She was bouncing on that motherfucker like a pogo stick.

Jealousy easily filled me.

Kilmya never got wild with me like that. Watching her now brought me to the realization that those times together was nothing more than a duty. Come to think of it, I was always the one doing the pursuing....other than that one time.

The first time I met Noonie.

Shaking my head, trying to rid myself of the sordid memory, I looked at the couple on my bed, then went to my closets to dress.

Noonie had killed my mood and Kilmya introduced me to the real side of her tonight with Remy. I'll let them have this one, but I *will* remind this entire island who I am. Tatum will not remain Chief and the young Mistress Jameria will not live to see her spawn born.

I will get my title back as Chief and if I don't.......I will die trying, taking some of these motherfuckers with me.

Chapter 12

Nuieve..........

"Did she go to Motif's chambers?"

"Yes. She did everything you said she would do. My guard also informed me Motif's right-hand man is still in his suite," Marlease said, shaking his head. The youngest elder in our history, still trying to wrap his head around secrets that were unbeknownst to him until today.

"I'm sorry my young friend for having to involve you in this mess, but Vilmander was my best friend and also Chief and Elder of this Island, until he took his last breath. His dying wish was to make his first born grandson claim his seat as heir of Geri. Motif was never meant to be Chief," I said, staring in his unbelievable eyes.

He raised his glass of cognac to his lips with a shaky hand, taking two long gulps. After a moment, he finally asked the question that mattered. "How in the hell did Motif manage to stay Chief the first four years of Tatum's life? Ky was still alive. She could've had Motif kicked off this island the day Tatum was born."

"Simple my young friend," I said, feeling nothing but sadness as I lay this burden on his shoulders. "Guilt. Guilt kept her quiet. She sacrificed her life because of it. Two years after Tatum's birth, Vilmander came to me about Ky's secret. He said she had come to him for help and he was the only person she could tell who

Tatum's biological father is. At first Vilamander was furious. But after he finished his tyrant of revelations, he was smiling.

I asked him why was he so happy? 'Ky just told me Tatum is fathered by another man.' His smile widen. Vilmander came to me and grabbed my shoulders, looking me in my eyes as he said, 'and he is also chief of this Island. Motif has no bloodlines with us. He can no longer rob our people. He can return back to the salvage land he came from,' he said with wide excited eyes. Once I understood, my next question was, what exactly did Ky need help with. He told me the guilt was eating away at her and that she wanted to end this farce and give Motif the child he deserved.

"Once Vilmander and I talked about it, he went to Ky, asking her about Tatum's father whereabouts. Either it was, she really didn't know or she just wasn't going to tell him, anyway. It was obvious that she was still in love with the guy." Marlease stood pacing. This was too much to take in. "Look Marlease, how about we pick this up some other--."

"No. I'm fine," he said still pacing. Then he stopped. "What did Vilmander do?"

I got up, took a sip of my drink before going to my desk and retrieving several pictures from a hidden drawer. I place a stack on top of the desk. He came and picked up the one with a young Tatum sitting on Vilmander shoulders and beautiful a Ky looking up at her son, smiling proudly.

"Vilmander forgave her and they spent the last year and six months of his life trying to find Tatum's father together."

His eyes snapped up from the picture, knowing there was more. "What happened?"

"Motif and his pack spent a lot of time on the mainland when they weren't traveling from one place to another, so we could never keep up with his comings and goings. Out of the ordinary, Motif went to his wife chambers to greet her and walked in quietly on a conversation her and Vilmander was having.

"Vilmander told me Motif was ranting and raving about why his wife would not lay with him. Betrayal and lies. In the mist of all the arguing, Vilmander let it slip that Tatum will be Chief of this island once they've found his real father. Vilmander died not long after that. The autopsy said he died from heart failure. But I and a few other people figured Motif had something to do with it."

When I looked back at Marlease, he was sitting in a chair with his head in his hands.

He finally looked up from the long moment of silence. "How did he get her to have Boaz," he asked with fierce bright eyes.

I walked back to my desk, placing the pictures and a set of keys with a map inside a white envelope and walked it over to him. He stared at it like it was the end of his life.

"Soon after the death of Vilmander, Ky withdrew within herself. She had no one to confide in and Motif made it difficult for me to get to her. When Motif was informed the Elders in training was returning home to be wedded, he went to Council and informed us he was taking Ky on a get-a-way to cheer her up. I had no idea he only said that to get her away from Demarcus.

"I finally had the chance to talk to Ky, when Motif went to the mainland with his pack for a going away party. I snuck in her room that night determined to talk to her. To get her to trust me. I told her everything Vilmander entrusted in me and with surprised teary eyes, she ran into my arms letting her tears soak my shoulder," I said with tears in my own eyes.

As Marlease took the envelope and placed it inside his jacket pocket, I walked back to my window, keeping a cool eye on Motif's chambers as I continued.

"She said she was already pregnant, but she wasn't trying to save herself. Just her son. 'I need you to make sure Demarcus takes care of Tatum, but you cannot tell him about his real father,' she said. I was shocked and asked her why. She smiled and said that Demarcus would do the right thing and go and find Tatum's father, no matter the consequences. She just wanted to make sure that Tatum is not harmed by Motif, once she left this earth.

"In the envelope I gave you, is not for your eyes, but for the Mistress. For Jameria."

"Jameria? I don't understand?"

I smiled with my back still to him, watching Noonie leave Motif's quarters. "She's pregnant Marlease. And I think they're running, because either they're scared or looking for a loophole. In that envelope is Jameria's loophole."

Motif had just left his quarters.

"I hate to end this conversation so soon, but I'm afraid other duties call." I hugged him at the door and asked him to take the front entrance. "I'm sorry to put this burden on you, but you are the only one I can trust with this other than Demarcus."

"I understand. Demarcus is where he should be....Protecting our kids."

I didn't bother to close my chamber doors after he left. Soon I heard my unguarded south hall doors opening and closing tightly behind someone. I went to my bar, washing out the glass Marlease had just used and placed it back in the cupboard.

"Care for a drink, Motif?"

"Of course. How about we do it like the old days," he said locking the door. "Haven't been in this office in a while. Didn't know you got it redone."

I grabbed two gold shot glasses and the tequila from the bar, joining him on the sofa. "Do you really want to talk about my decorating skills or is there something else that caused this visit," I said passing him a glass.

He gulped it down and fixed himself another. "That's what I like about you, Nuieve. You're always to the point." He gulped another glass down before sitting back on the couch unbuckling his pants and pulling his huge dick out, jacking himself and slapping it against his hand. "How about you suck on this, while I tell you about it."

I took my own gulp, letting it burn my throat before I leaned over and started sucking on the head. He pushed his pants further down so I could play with his balls while sucking him off.

"I wanted to remind you of this dirty little secret of yours, if you're thinking about betraying me....Oh that feels good. Do you know how Council will act if they found out the eldest Elder on council is gay?"

I didn't say anything. I just kept on sucking.

"I'm not going to lie though......oh.....you sure do give good head for an old guy."

He flipped me over and started pounding my head in the couch, almost chocking me to death.

"Yeah.......suck this dick, bitch."

His powerful dick was pumping hard against my jaws. My dick got instantly hard on its' own accord.

After his first nut, he was dragging me up by my long salt and pepper hair. He got right in my face as his cum dripped from my lips. "How would you feel to have everything stripped away from you, because a bitch lied?"

I grinned in his face. My mouth full of semen and spit. "I don't know," I replied. "Tell me."

He slapped me several times and started tearing my tailor-made-to-fit off of me.

"Fucking cunt," he yelled, as he tore my shirt from my shoulders, sending buttons flying everywhere. "If I find out you plotted against me, I'll fuck you up so bad, the entire island will think the 'Red Light District' moved up in your ass." He stood over my bruised aching body with his long stiff dong hanging over my head. "Assume the position, bitch. And this time, I hope you cleaned yourself out. Don't want no mishaps like the last time."

I stood, removing the rest of my torn expensive clothes and climbed on the couch with my head and hands resting on the back of the sofa and my ass in the air.

Motif showed me no mercy.

He entered me hard, raw, and to the hilt. I pushed back against him, sucking his dick deeper in my anus. The head of my own dick began throbbing, painfully aching for release. Motif gripped me by my hair, slammed me down and began fucking me in the missionary position. I

grabbed my own dick and began to jackoff as he pumped continuously in my ass. I raised, my hips higher, resting my heels on his chest, giving him better access.

He drilled in me with ferocity. All his anger showing in his powerful thrusts.

He came hard, filling my deep hole with his hot thick cum. Hot jism from my own penis, drizzled down the sides before a volcano shot forward, spraying us both.

He snatched his pipe from my ass. "Even rape gets your gay ass off. Tell me one thing, you backwards slut. Do you know anything about Jameria's pregnancy?"

I think I showed the right amount of surprise, because I didn't think Motif would find out so soon.

From the look on my face, he followed the wrong impression. "Well, its obvious Council don't know anything about it from the look on your face. So I tell you what, you keep in mind that I keep that dirty little secret about you and your deceased wife and you forget I asked you that question about our dear little Mistress and Chief. I'll bring it to Council myself when I'm ready to expose the leading couple."

He took my designer boxers, wiped his long penis off and threw them on me like a cheap hoe, before he walked out of the door.

I picked my tattered clothes up off the floor before heading to my sleeping chambers to bath and dress.

As the water peddled against my back, I thought about what Motif said. He knows Jameria's pregnant. If he tell the Council board before Tatum announce it, it will surely be bad for the young couple……and my plans to reunite with Cassandra will be over Motif's dead body.

I dressed down in all white linen attire and exit on bare feet from my private garden door. The lights to the visitors' quarters were still on. Pineacia and her daughters were mingling with islanders earlier. I entered the hall through the private entrance, making sure I was not seen. I peeped through the thick burgundy curtains that separated the dining area from the sitting room and saw Pineacia entertaining one of our diplomats and his wife. I closed the curtain tightly and crossed the dining room, heading straight for the servant quarters.

I tapped lightly on the door. Cassandra opened it immediately with a huge smile on her face.

"I thought you weren't going to show. What kept you?"

I never told her about Motif blackmailing me. Only that he knows our secret and that we could never marry. "I was waiting for your Mistress to retire for the evening. How long do she plans to stay," I asked.

She came to me, circling her arms around my neck. "She was planning to stay long enough for the royal couple to return. She wants to make an arranged marriage with their first born child to her unborn grandchild."

"What?"

"Don't look so surprised my love. Because your Council is lenient and let your young Chief choose his own bride does not mean that goes for all of us. Geri Island is home to not only treasure, but gifted royals. Leaders from all over will be vying for the young couples first born. As long as they've been on their honeymoon, I'm quite sure she has a bun in the oven as we speak," she said, smiling.

God. If she only knew.

"I'm sure the entire pack is enjoying their time away. But the short time I have with you, I want to spend it on us. Not them."

I pulled her long silk robe apart, letting my eyes feast on her masterpiece.

Long slim cinnamon body, long sandy brown hair with perfect breast, tapered muscled waist and a thick long dong.

My Cassandra was born with tits and a third leg.

"Are you ready for me baby," she said, stroking her pole.

"More than," I replied, grabbing her, dominating her Botox filled lips.

Once Cassandra hit fifty, mid-life crisis seem to take over her entire being. I almost didn't recognize her at the wedding. But no matter what she did to her face, her perfect body stayed in contact. Kissing her ferociously, I guided her back until she tumbled on the bed. I took my time licking and sucking the length of her body until I made it to the prize. I took her deep in my mouth in one long stroke.

"Yesss.....just like that daddy. Damn, you have some sweet lips."

She removed the rubber band from my long hair, wrapping both of her hands in it, using it as reigns before she started pumping, hitting my uvula with a pleasurable force. I released her fun sick and went straight for her heavy sensitive sack. With the first flick of my tongue, she came with a vengeance. I shot up, determined to catch every last drop of her essence. She twitched and trembled with delight as I savored her sweetness.

"My turn," she announced breathlessly.

She tackled me, pushing me flat on my back, removing my pants while I wrestle the linen shirt from my body. Reciprocating what I did to her, she added two fingers to the mix, messaging my loose anus. The sensations were intense as her head bobbed faster, creating friction with her mouth.

"Damn, I missed you," I said as she added a third finger to join the other two. "I wish you would never leave me."

She rose up on her hunches, releasing me completely and giving me a toothy grin. Her injected lips was wet and glossy from the spit shine she did to my dick. "Maybe after your new leading couple return, a few changes will be made."

Boy, if she only *knew*! "Actually, I'm depending on it." I saw confusion in her blue-green eyes. Before she could ask the question, I brought it back to us. "Enough about them. Us, remember?"

She smiled again, raising from her hunches and squatted over my Johnson. She rolled and rotated her ass to the classic jazz music, playing in the background.

Thanks to Motif, I didn't bust my first nut with her until after she came twice, coating my abdomen with her thick cream.

"Damn baby. You're extremely relaxed," she said, after we switched positions with me on top stroking her glory stick with my anus. "Did you jackoff before meeting me?"

I smiled down at her rotating my hips, sucking her deeper inside me. "I'm an old man. I'll do what I have to, to make the moment last." Then I leaned forward, taking a round ripe tit in my mouth while bouncing my ass on her dick at the same time.

She came so hard, she started speaking in tongues. So much cum shot up my ass, felt like I received an enema. It drained down her pole like a melting ice cream cone.

Before I could savor the feel of her coating my ass, that special ring came. Tatum.

My phone rung twice more, before it went silent again. I was out of the bed within seconds, trying to put my clothes on all at once.

"Slow down baby, before you hurt yourself. Is that phone call *that* important," she asked. Suspicion coloring her words.

"It's not like that. You know there is no one else for me, but you. Yet, you are right. The call is very important. How about I tell you about it tomorrow, over dinner?"

She smiled. It's been months since I've seen that smile. "Sure. Of course, it has to be a private dinner. You know the rules," she said with a slight shrug.

But I'm hoping to change that.

The unique ringtone filled the room again. "We'll talk over dinner. Please excuse my sudden parting, but I must take this," I said, kissing her cheek, then heading straight for the door.

I jogged to the back exit and answered before voicemail caught it.

"Hello?"

"Hello, Elder Nuieve," said the smooth tenor voice. "We need to talk."

"Yes we do, but not right now. I'm heading back to my chambers as we speak."

"Fine. How is everyone, by the way?"

I laughed indignantly. "Do you really care?"

"What kind of question is that?"

I entered my suite from the garden's end, locking the patio doors before speaking again. "Because, people who care don't run."

"Is that what you think we're doing," he said, his smooth voice going down an octave.

"I don't know. You tell me."

He ignored the statement, asking a question of his own. "Where's Boaz?"

Did Motif tell Boaz the truth about Tatum's parentage? "How would I know? He left with you and your pack."

There was a moment of silence before he spoke again. "He's no longer a part of my pack. Him and his mate was challenged," he said as a-matter-of-fact…..and nothing more.

"What?!" God, the worse *has* happened. "Boaz is no longer a part of your pack? What the hell do you mean challenge? Who challenged him?"

Another moment of silence, before he said, "Me."

I was struck dumb beyond words.

Before I could respond, he continued. "Jameria sent him and Shy to Tibet to train with the monks, but uncle Demarcus said they'd checked out a few hours after their arrival. I really don't care about his whereabouts, but a few of the pack members want to have a word with him."

A moment passed before I asked my next question. "Tatum, is Motif the reason you and Boaz had a fallen out?"

"Part of it. Look Elder Nu-"

"Tatum wait. There's something I have to tell you." I took a deep breath and let it out. "Motif is not your real father."

"I know." As he explained the course of events that took place after they departed, the blood seem to drain from my body like Cassandra's thick nut drained from my ass, soaking my linen pants. "But," he continued. "What does who my father is, have to do with this? And why are you so involved?"

From the tone of his voice, asking for favors would not be a good idea right now. "Your grandfather Vlimander, was my leader and my friend. I was the only person he trusted with his secrets. *And I trusted him with all of my secrets also,* I wanted to add.

"What has that got to do with anything? Are you *trying* to confuse me, Elder?"

God, I wish I could be as honest with him as I'd been within myself decades ago. "Tatum, I know you don't trust me enough to believe that I'm on your side. Just believe me when I say, I am. I think I might know what Motif is up to and I know you're struggling, trying to find a loophole for the 'Birthing Ritual.' I gave Marlease all of the information you might need.....How is Jameria, anyway?"

Another bout of silence. "She's fine. Going into her fourth month. How did you know?"

I actually laughed at his surprise.

"Tatum, a woman who is as head strong as about seeing the world is bound and determined to do the right thing. Even if it cost her all of her hopes and dreams," I said going into the bathroom. The back of my linen pants were soaked and I couldn't stand it any longer. "Seriously though, the people are getting restless without their leading couple. When will you be home?" I have to be careful and mindful of what I say.

Motif has ears everywhere.

"We don't know yet." He took a deep breath before he continued. "We just found out Kalanie, Cougar, Tyce, and Maria are all pregnant, too."

"Already?" Did they plan these pregnancies? A whole new scene played before my eyes. "All of you left on your honeymoon a few weeks ago. Did the rest of the pack know Jameria was already with child?"

Another quiet moment before he responded. "No. Just a coincidence."

I knew it was a lie before it left his lips.

My God. What has Tatum done?

A cold chill went through me, raising the hair on the back of my neck. In that moment, I was actually afraid.

"Tatum, did you ever think of what your child will become? Jameria is a snake charmer. A beautiful one at that, who has a gift that goes beyond the ordinary. Have you considered what the baby will become?" I didn't won't to say, *especially if your wife don't make it through the birthing process, that is.*

"Don't worry about it, Elder. We'll be back to make the announcement in a couple of months. Just keep it quiet until then," he said.

At the same time he answered, I heard a bump on the other side of the door."I understand. There's a lot more I wish I could tell you, but unfortunately, I'm not in a comfortable position to discuss it over the phone. Have a safe journey home." I didn't bother waiting for a response.

I clicked off my phone, removed the rest of my soiled clothes and put on a terry cloth robe, before leaving the bathroom.

Relaxing in my favorite recliner with nothing on but a skimpy pair of thongs was my 28 year old wife, Kilmya. I didn't bother to greet her as I made my way to the bar.

"Care for a drink," I asked her as I poured myself a gin and tonic.

"How about some of that load that's oozing out of your ass, making a puddle around your feet." She stood from the recliner, removing her six inch stilettos and pranced her ass over to me. "I heard you mumbling on the phone. Who was you talking to?"

"None of your damn business," I said nonchalantly. The worse mistake I ever made was marrying her. Not only was she young enough to be my granddaughter, but she's also old enough to be accountable for the mess she got herself in.

"Come to bed," she said, removing a cube of ice from my glass. "I feel like being a wife tonight."

"You mean all that dick Motif shoved in you was not enough." Turning my back on her, I walked to the king size bed not bothering to remove my robe.

I decided to wait until she left to go to one of her men for the night, before heading to the shower. Most likely, she'll find my anus extremely loose and still sticky with Cassandra's sweet nut.

"Was it enough for you? I know Motif's been packing that ass a few times. He likes to brag about it when he's fucking me."

I shook my head. Stupid bitch. "Don't you have no shame? I'm still your husband Kilmya. Keep your shit to yourself and I'll do the same." When she opened her mouth to say something else, I slammed me glass down and went back to the bathroom to shower.

I stood under the hot water, letting it beat against my skin. My thoughts drifted to my conversation with Tatum. Motif must've told Boaz the truth. What other reason would Tatum have to challenge Boaz, unless the boy was after the title of Chief....but he would be giving up his position as Jameria's left-hand. And if he gave it up, who did Tatum pick to take his place? Being the left-hand of the Mistress is a duty people kill to have. Other than the Chief, the Mistress left-hand man is the closest to her. So close that it's almost intimate. The main rule is to protect the Mistress at all cost. Would Boaz really give up a chance like that?

"Let me help you clear your thoughts, love." Kilmya stepped in the shower behind me and placed her soft hands on my back. "Do you mind?"

"You're in here now. Go right ahead."

She began to message my shoulders as she spoke. "Motif hired assassins to takeout the Mistress, but each one they hire comes up missing. Boaz doesn't know that Tatum is his half-brother and

Noonie's been snooping around Jameria's parents for what reason, I have no clue."

My confusion and curiosity spiked was at an all-time high now. "I don't understand. Why are you telling me this? Why help me when I know for a fact that you don't want to be here," I asked facing her.

Her hands fell from my shoulders to her sides. "Because you and your people isn't the only ones Motif fucked over. He literally stole my family's island from right under their noses, then went about searching our land for treasure. Forcing almost all of my people into poverty. The only way I can help them is by retrieving those documents back from him. Bu now that there's a new Chief, I'm going to need all of the help I can get." She paused for a moment to get control of her emotions, before she continued. "I'm sorry for marrying you under false pretense. I should never had lied and said I was pregnant with your child. I'm sorry, but I'll do anything for my people."

I pulled her close, hugging her tightly. Understanding her more now than in the last five years I'd her husband. "We'll do all we can to see it happen. But once your family receive their home back, what will you do? You know there is no such thing as divorce on this island."

Her face lit up like a rainbow. "Since I'm married to such a lenient man, I decided to spend a few months on my homeland with a young fellow I grew up with. I don't know much about the new leading couple, but I think they will help me since all of us is in the same boat together. And I know you're dying to be with your Cassandra."

Kilmya understood more than I gave her credit for. But there's still a lot I can't trust her with, yet. "How did you know about Tatum's parentage?" The one and only thing I know about Kilmya is that she never lied to me about anything, other than the time she claim to be pregnant.

But even then, she came forward a couple days after the wedding, begging me for forgiveness.

"Motif tried to pump me for information a few times during pillow talk. He told me a lot of your island's secrets, including the fact that you're bi-sexual, but I already knew that," she said lathering her body. Her perky tits were small compared to Cassandra's, but quite the size for a woman with such a small frame. "Anyway, what Motif didn't know was the Mistress is with child. He beat the shit out of his right-hand man just for mentioning it."

Wow.

Jameria's pregnancy really has Motif on edge. Knowing the girl have to go through the traditional 'Birthing Ritual,' should make him that happiest man in the world. But the child she leaves behind, if she should die, will be Motif's new problem. Is it possible he wants her gone so bad, he would risk his own grandchild? But it wouldn't be his grandchild....not biologically. And there's no doubt Motif is trying to reclaim his title as

Chief.......so his own seed can succeed him. So the real question is, where is Boaz?

Chapter 13

Tatum.........

I stood beside my Mistress with the rest of my pack behind us, watching our island rise from mysterious waters. Bittersweet memories clouding my mind. Jameria squeezes my hand, taking me away from my melancholy thoughts. No time to reminisce.

We have a lot of work to do.

"Do you think Demarcus made it home already?" Tyvine and the rest of my brothers were on edge.

Once I told them we had to go back to the island, they almost strung my ass from an old oak tree.

"No. He won't be back for a while."

I watched Tyvine put his hand on Cougar's slight bulge. His head bowed as if he was praying as hard as he could.

I walked over to him, placing my hand on his shoulder. "Everything will be fine Ty. I promise."

He looked at me with hopeful tears in his eyes. "I pray you're right Tatum. Because if anything happens to my wife, you'll hate me for burning that motherfucker down, he said," his head jerking towards the island.

I smiled. "In that case, I'll let you stand by my side and watch it sink, because if something happens to your family that will mean something happen to mine first."

He moved further away from his mate. His smile more sinister now. "Then how about we skip the formalities Chief and just take these bitches out. Let's get rid of the whole fucking island," he said in a deep sultry voice. Like he's caressing the idea.

"We can't do that," said Cole. "We can't just destroy the entire island."

"Fuck that! Everybody is doing their best to guarantee our mates go through this birthing bullshit. Why the fuck did we come back anyway. Let's just exile ourselves and get the fuck away from here."

Jameria stepped forward. The three of us parted, bowing our heads, letting our long hair shade our faces as her pretty bare feet came into view.

She placed soft fingers tips under Tyvine's smooth chiseled chin, raising his face to meet her honey brown eyes. "We're going home Tyvine. Home to a place where we are leaders of. Motif is running around terrorizing our people. We have to go show him who we are and that *we* own this bitch. And not even a pregnancy will stop us from coming."

Tyvine smiled, staring deep into her eyes before he leaned down kissing her softly on her lips. "Please forgive me Mistress," he said taking both of her small hands into his. "The pass few months actually felt like a dream. Just my brothers and our mates......My family. No looking over our shoulders wondering who's trying to kill us next."

Silence. Then laughter erupted.

"That's because no one was trying to kill us in Louisiana. No one knew where we were going, but me. Anyway, I'm glad all of you enjoyed my grandma's farm."

Jameria had Pat Ann's little shack re-done into a three story farm house with a wrap-a-round porch on the upper and lower levels. She purchased the rest of the land surrounding the house, leaving most of the foliage and trees for privacy. The fourteen bedroom, ten bath home didn't have all the amenities as our palace, but the peace, quietness, and the dream of living a quiet life in the bayou, was too much to be true.

Tyvine was right. It felt just like a dream I could live in forever.

I watched my mate as the wind blew through her wavy black hair. Her white sundress blowing against her swollen milk filled breasts. With her cloak hanging from my hands, I covered her placing my now free hands on her round belly, saying a silent prayer before leaving the boat.

"I wish you and the girls had listen to me and stayed in the States," I said, my forehead resting against hers. "You smiled more back in the States.

"Did you think I would be smiling with my husband and brothers so far away, about to go to battle with an idiot and his stupid followers," she tsked, tilting her lovely head to the side mockingly. "Why do boys want to have all the fun for themselves?"

I kissed her softly at first, then aggressively. More possessive. It was so hard tearing my lips from hers, but I need to get her and the rest of the women inside without being seen.

Tyvine, Moham, Karden, and Cole cloaked themselves also, after helping their wives. Pierce and Carmen descended first, being as quiet as a mouse. We arrived at the island right at nightfall, blending our yacht with the rest in the harbor. We moved quickly through the courtyard, heading straight for Demarcus wing of the palace. As planned, his suite of rooms will be our domain until he returns. The only faces the rest of the islanders will see is mine, Karden and Tyvine's. Cole, Moham, and Pierce will stay with the women.

"I don't know if I can do this man. I've never been away from Cougar for a long period of time."

"Damn, Tyvine. They're right here on the island with us. Right in our reach. You need to calm down man," Karden said, patting him on his back. "I think you spent too many months without your girls' gift being active. The States made you soft," he continued laughing.

The women had no real use for their gifts in the States. Jameria's snakes stayed close to us, while living on the farm, but stayed in the back pond. There was no danger. After the death of Jameria's grandmother a few of her hometown people started accepting her (without her knowledge). There were rumors about Jameria while she was living on the island. Her people assumed someone had harmed her and her grandmother died from a broken heart. Only a few people knew the truth; that her grandmother sent her away for a better life.

"Here," Kelanie said, placing the thick blunt in his hand. "You need to smoke that before you leave. We can't let you fuck this up for us, Tyvine. You hold a new position now. Smoke and mellow the fuck out."

Cole passed him a lighter.

"Go in the bathroom with that, baby. Demarcus might have a fit if he smelled herb burning in his place."

"Come with me," he said, grabbing Cougar's hand.

"Do they have to leave tonight? Cougar's a lot calmer with Tyvine. We're the ones who's going to suffer while he's away." Tyce was practically asleep in Moham's lap. It was obvious my pack wasn't ready to leave the comforts of Jameria's Cajun land.

"They can't risk being seen leaving Demarcus place. People might come snooping. Besides all of this will be over once Tatum makes the announcement," Moham said, stroking her cheek.

"I'm going to bed," Jameria announced.

I followed her to her personal bedroom Demarcus had custom made just for her in his suit.

Her entire room was done in peanut butter and chocolate. Her favorite colors. The bronze silk comforter and the cream colored sheets was already turned down. She strolled bare feet on thick cream carpet to her closet, removing the white satin baby doll gown.

"Are you alright," I asked circling my arms around her round belly caressing her stomach.

"I'm fine. Just feeling sorry for the rest of the pack." She leaned back into me, placing her hands on top of mine.

Guilt laid so heavy on my heart. "I'm so sorry I did this. Especially to you......I don't think I'll ever be able to forgive myself."

She turned all of a sudden, taking my face between her hands. "There's nothing to feel guilty about. What's done is done."

I kissed her softly, stooping and lifting her in my arms effortlessly. I carried her to the bed, laying her down gently. "There's something I have to have before leaving you."

My lips dominated hers.

She placed her small hands on my biceps as I deepened the kiss. My hands working her cotton dress up and over her head, taking in her beautiful bronze skin. I began to kiss a trail down her neck, drowning in her deep throaty moans, as my hands massaged and caressed her milk filled breasts. My tongue licked and laved her left nipple, drinking down her mothers'nectar while I played havoc with her right breast as more milk covered my hand.

Knock. Knock. Knock. "Come on Tatum. You gotta go."

Sometimes my brothers really gets on my nerves. "Get the fuck away from the door, Cole!"

Giggling, Jameria said, "Please go. I don't won't him busting in here. He can be an ass sometimes.

I sighed deeply. "Okay. But this shit has gotta stop. I understand we're a pack and all, but we're just too damn close."

"Well, after I have this baby...and if I live to see it, a couple of us will be closer than that. Will you be able to handle it?"

Jameria told me about the conversation between her and Boaz. From the little information we could gather from uncle Demarcus, there's a book for the eyes of the Mistresses personal servant only. The book had only been used a couple of times since there was only two Mistresses in our entire existence. If what Boaz said is true, then my decision have to be sound. My uncle told me Motif was furious he could not change Ky's left-hand man. At the time he chose Elder Marlease wife, since they were so close. He didn't know the details until after my mother gave birth to me.

"Baby, my decision was made when you told me what Bo said. My choice will probably put my little brother in the mental institution, but that's not my fault. I just hope *he* can handle it," I said kissing her.

She smiled at me confused. "What are you talking about? Who did you pick?"

I looked up at her still drinking from her tit. "The only other person he's more afraid of than me."

She thought a moment, then burst out laughing. "You are so cruel."

I laughed myself, but got serious realizing time was whining down. "Let me taste you baby. Please."

I crawled down between her legs lapping up her sweet juices, determined to bust a nut before leaving up out this bitch.

Her orgasm had her arching belly and all from the bed. She shook like an earthquake trying to break the Richter scale.

Someone started beating on the door again. I leaned over the side of the bed, grabbing one of my shoes and threw it, hitting the door. "Get the fuck away from the door!" More giggles from the other side.

I ignored them, lying on my side now, completely naked behind my wife. I took my time, being as gentle as possible as I entered her. My hips rolled and pumped smoothly as I caressed her swollen breasts. More of her mothers' milk spilled over my fingers. Being mindful not to push my fourteen inch pole to the hilt, I placed my hand on her stomach to remind me not to go King Kong on the pussy. My libido was at an all-time high and jacking off was no cutting it. Blowjobs and hand-jobs from my wife was a tease. After the fourth or fifth nut of the day, I still be hornier than a jackrabbit.

I thought these new feelings was me coming of age, until I found out Jameria puts 'maca root' in our food whenever she cooks. The one secret we didn't know about our Mistress……. Just like the magic she creates with her food, she express the same feeling with me. Her soft moans and urgent cries with each thrust always have me on the edge of exploding.

She fell asleep in my arms afterwards.

A black cobra lay curled in a corner of the bedroom. I slid from her embrace, letting my bare feet sink into the soft plush carpet. He came to me instantly. I went to him quickly, bending to let him curl around my arm. I went to the window he came through, releasing him from my arm. He slithered into a nest of oncoming snakes.

I released a deep sigh before trotting back to the bed to wake my wife, yet again.

She stirred, slowly stretching her limbs. "What is it?"

"Your welcoming party is here," I said, pulling her silk robe from the closet.

She sighed, plopping her hands down on the bed beside her in exasperation. "Three months without that, was not enough."

"I know. But in a few more months, you'll be a free woman. Can you bear with it until then?" During the beginning of Jameria's pregnancy, our bedroom was no longer a safe place to lay our heads. Because of the constant threat of danger and the snakes' protectiveness of the baby, we had to spend most of our nights in the snake pit. It was the only way to keep them from invading the palace.

It took us a while to figure out the threat was in my own fucking pack. Worse, the threat was my blood brother. Boaz.

"Fine. But I'm not staying all night in that damn pit. I'll make sure one of the guys come and retrieve me after about an hour or two."

After she dressed down in her beige silk pajama set and downed her silk robe, I got dressed myself to at least walk her to the jungle's edge.

When we entered Demarcus sitting room, Tyvine and Karden was already cloaked and waiting.

With crimson red eyes Tyvine kissed his wife forehead after kissing all of his sisters' cheeks. "No cat play while I'm gone," he joked kissing her lips lightly. She circled her arms around his neck, lifting on tip toes and sliding her tongue in his mouth. He grabbed a handful of curly red hair angling her head slightly as his tongue dove deep in her mouth, reciprocating the gesture.

"Stop," I said walking to the front door. "The last thing I want to see is you and Cougar's free spirited asses fucking in front of us, again. Come on. We're going to walk the Mistress a little ways to the pit, before going to the Elder's wing."

"Don't worry about it. I'll walk her down. Now might be the one and only chance I get to talk to my dad." Pierce was dreading this moment. It was the call he received from his father that brought us back here. He pleaded with us to let him come here alone, but there was no way in hell I was going to lose another pack brother.....besides the other few chain of calls that came right after, had us packing the next day.

"Are you sure Pierce? You can wait until the announcement. What's one more day," Jameria said. She was so protective of my 17 year old pack

brother. After the damage Bo and Shy did on him and his mate, I thought I would be losing four members, instead of two. But when Carmen came to Jameria begging to leave the island, so many unanswered questions started falling into place, showing us the real Boaz. My strange dreams were more like premonitions after the long talks and counseling we had to do with the two. So much about my little brother I'm still having trouble believing.

"I'm fine, Mistress," he said, kissing her cheek. "I'm a much stronger man, now. Stop worrying about me."

"But-," she started to protest.

"But nothing. What happened to me and Carmen was nothing out of the ordinary that a lot of kids go through. But like *you* said. It's my choice if I let it make me or break me. Now, can we please leave before you fall into one of your crying spells?"

She couldn't help but smile, remembering her episodes of emotional breakdowns.

Carmen stood and kissed his lips softly. "Be careful. It would be best if you stayed at your father's until dawn. That way you can walk back with the Mistress."

We downed our black silk cloaks, walking out of the sitting room.

Demarcus wing was shut off from anyone with prying eyes. His personal courtyard was bolted down and bricked connecting to the cherry oak double doors of his outer wing. He had ten rooms on his hall, each with its' own sitting room, bathroom, and garden. We walked down the long corridor, moving with sturdy precision unlatching the thick medieval doors. The night air was cool and moist. Just before we separated, I pulled Jameria to the side for one last kiss.

"Be careful. I'll miss you."

She smiled up at me. "You as well."

I watched Pierce and Jameria duck off in the jungle from our sight.

"We should've stayed in the bayou." Tyvine just wouldn't let it go.

"I didn't become Chief to run from my obligations, Ty. Anyway, this is not a permanent stay. After we get a few things straight and take care of our business with Council, we're leaving."

"Going where." Karden was the first one to volunteer to stay behind. I had to practically drag his ass from the secluded farmhouse. "Motif probably knows about that place now. We can't go back there."

I don't have time for this. "We'll talk about that later," I said walking ahead of them.

I wanted to stay in the States just as bad as they did, but if I can't get them to see the dilemma I'm in, how can I actually call myself a good Chief? I've procrastinated too long not telling them about my parentage. Not wanting them to see me as a different person. But how else can I get them to understand if Motif or Boaz gets their hands on Jameria before she gives birth. My reign will be over before it begins.

We entered Nuieve's private garden before I turned to my two pack brothers.

"There's something I have to tell you." They both stared at me waiting. I took a deep breath before spilling the truth. "Motif is not my father." And then there was silence.

Chapter 14

Karden............

Okay. What am I supposed to say at a time like this?

Fuck it. I'll just ask him.

"Umm, Tatum. Am I supposed to say congratulations or I'm sorry?"

"I don't even need to think about it, man. Congratulations! He's not your father," Tyvine said, clapping Tatum on the back.

I had so many questions, I didn't know where to begin. "How do you know," was the obvious.

"I'll tell you about it, but first things first."

Without thought, we all looked at Elder Nuieve's door to his private garden. Tatum entered first, using the side window. Nuieve kept his entire wing locked except for the window that was furthest down from the door with its' broken latch. Tyvine went next then I came in last, closing the window behind me.

Tatum didn't bother to cut on the lights.

He knew the room well.

Elder Nuieve gave Jameria this room as her own personal room in his wing, like the rest of the elders.

Before he could turn the latch, I said, "Wait. Do you hear that?"

We stood quiet for a moment. Then we heard it again.

A man moaning in pleasure.

Tyvine asked, "Is that Nuieve?"

Well that's a surprise. I didn't think him and Kilmya were intimate with each other. After she confessed to him that she wasn't pregnant he vowed never to touch her again.

We tiptoed out of the room and down the hall in our black cloaks. Nuieve's private sitting room door was open. Tyvine closed and locked it behind him after the three of us entered.

The grunting and groaning of two people being intimate echoed throughout the room.

"Swallow the whole thing, baby."

We looked at each other in shock. Was Nuieve having a threesome?

Tyine mouth, "I didn't know the old dog still had it in him." He moved to the bedroom door against Tatum's insistence not to, and slowly opened the door enough to get a glimpse. But whatever he saw had him back tracking and bumping into me. He hurriedly exited the sitting room again, leaving me and Tatum in total confusion. We followed him out, closing the door behind me.

"What is it," Tatum whispered.

Tyvine glanced at him and shook his head with a look of total disgust on his face.

Tatum came to the wrong conclusion and was about to go back in when Tyvine caught him by his shoulder. "Don't. Not what you think."

"Then what is it," I asked. My patience was running thin.

He just couldn't bring himself to say the words. He just closed his eyes and bowed his head.

This time Tatum went to the door. But instead of cracking it an inch, he threw the motherfucker wide open.

Like Tyvine, I was beyond speechless. I wish I could dig my eyes out and sooth them. Tell them everything is going to be alright. That it's not real.

Standing before us was a five foot seven inch island beauty with a dick. And to make matters worse, our elder, one of the oldest pack members alive, was on his knees sucking the hell out of it.

The chick with the dick looked up, finally noticing other people in the room. But the tripped out part is the bitch covered her tits, not her dick.

"Oh, my God," she said backing into the wall.

Nuieve swiveled his head around in a flash, laying shocked eyes on us. Before he could say a word, Tatum hurriedly slammed the door back.

"Wasn't expecting that shit." Tatum took a step back on wobbly legs.

"Told you," Tyvine said, shaking his lowered head.

"Actually, you didn't tell me shit. Because if you had, I probably wouldn't believe it! Shit. I'm having a hard time believing it now and I just saw the shit."

I came to my own conclusion. "Tatum, we need to get off of this fucking island. Now I know what Nuieve wanted when he was calling all over the world looking for you…."

As the words were leaving my mouth, it was already registering in Tatum's head. "Let's get the fuck outta here."

"Wait. Please." Nuieve was standing in his bedroom doorway, now dressed in a robe.

Thank God.

"So that's why you wanted me to rush back here? Motif's blackmailing you and you want me to help you."

"Yes Tatum, he's blackmailing me, but I'll let myself perish if it means saving Jameria and that baby."

"Jameria? What do she have to do with this? Stop fucking with me, Nuieve. You told me that you have information that is very important."

"Yes. But that info is for Jameria from your mom. Not for you."

"What?! I don't understand. What the fuck are you trying to say? Are you saying that my mother is ali-"

"No," Nuieve said walking to him. Tatum held up his hand and backed up a few paces like the man was contagious. Nuieve dropped his hands, went to his favorite lounge chair and let his body fall in it. "I don't know how to explain it. Maybe your mother had a premonition about it, but six months into her pregnancy with Boaz. Your mother gave me something. She told me to put it in the safest place I could think possible. She said I had to make sure only your wife lay eyes on it and that she'll know what to do from there.

"Not in my wildest dream did I ever think you would find a girl like Jameria. But your mother........your mother knew. I don't know how, but she knew. Her next words was, "'Tatum's wife is going to be someone very special, Nuieve. He will find her. Make sure it be Tatum who chooses his own mate and he *will* find her.'"

"What was it?" I couldn't help myself. "What did she leave Jameria?"

Nuieve turned his head slowly. "Wow. You boys gotten mighty close to let a pack member question an elder."

"Yes," Tyvine broke in. "We keep nothing from each other. It's not like we sit on a pedestal, judging other people lives, while *my* personal life is more disturb that others."

Nuieve looked to Tatum, waiting for him to chastise his pack brother for addressing an elder so. He only stared back at the man who looked more like a man of 40 instead of 60.

"Sometimes it's best to stay in your place and let your leader handle personal situations. There is some things that you *don't* know," he said, looking pointedly at Tatum.

Tyvine's smile was mischievous. "Like what? Like Motif was never the legitimate Chief of this Island? Like he can't take reign unless Tatum's entire bloodline cease to exist……That Motif is *not* his father?" Nuieve's mouth dropped open like he was about to give head again. "Like I said, we keep nothing from each other. Tatum is not Motif. Just answer the fucking question."

There was always something about Tyvine that intimidated people. Like Tatum, Tyvine is dangerous….on second thought. He's more dangerous than our Chief.

Nuieve shook his head. "Well, I wish I knew the answer to that question myself. She gave me a locked box wrapped in silk."

Tatum started pacing the room. Confusion coloring his face. "I don't get it. What makes you think my mother knew about Jameria before she died? It sounds like any mother-in-law who leaves mementoes behind."

Nuieve's eyes slowly rose to meet his. "Because the box was wrapped in Jameria's favorite color with her initials sewn into the fabric. For years I'd always wondered what the initials JB stood for, until the day I met Ms. Jameria Beau," he said in wonder.

I could see Tatum trying to put two and two together.

I asked Nuieve the questions that were necessary. "Where is the box?"

"I don't know," was his quick response.

"I thought you said you put it up for safe keeping." God. I hope Nuieve isn't lying to Ty. Elder or not, Tyvine is not the type to play too many word games.

Turning to Ty, he said, "She did, but I passed the package to another elder for safe keeping until *his* eyes lay upon our Mistress. Whatever is in that box, is for Jameria eyes only," he repeated.

"Well, Jameria isn't here," Tatum said, breaking out of his train of thought. "None of the girls are. We just came to make the announcement of our heirs. Karden and Tyvine will be representing Moham and Cole in their absence."

Nuieve didn't look surprised. "I'm guessing you left them behind to look after the women."

Tatum smiled. "It's hard to imagine someone like Cougar or Jameria as fragile, but at this stage we didn't want to take any chances." He sat back in his seat before he asked, "Who was that you were with Nuieve?"

At first, I didn't think he was going to answer, but moments later he must've came to the conclusion that it was inevitable. "Someone I loved way before Moham's father came into this world. Gerox was my youngest brother. He was arranged to marry the daughter of the Meeba tribe and he was also a candidate for Motif's pack. I met Cassandra at their wedding. It didn't dawn on me that she was the bride's sister until Gerox made the announcement of his son. Cassandra stayed on the island with her sister during tough periods of her pregnancy. The distance friendship between us eventually turned into something much more than either of us have ever asked for." He stood and went to his bar, pouring himself a gin and tonic. "I didn't know about Cassandra being a hermaphrodite, until my persistence for us to be intimate. She just blurted it out, waiting for me to run for the hills. But I found myself falling deeper and deeper in love with her.

"I even tried to get my father to call off my arranged marriage, but he wouldn't hear of it." He leaned back against the bar, swirling the cubed ice around in the glass. "So like any fool in love, I made a deal with the devil. I had my fiancé raped by Motif's wolf pack. Had her dishonored and band from this island and in the process lost my brother and sister-in-law, because of it."

"Why would Motif help you?"

"Because, at the time Demarcus comings and goings was very important to him."

"Demarcus?"

"Yes. The only person your mother trusted more than her own father."

194

"Why would Motif want to know who Demarcus was seeing? From my understanding, right after Cole was born and his wife died –"

"He devoted his life to his son and you at the time," Nuieve finished forhim. "Actually Motif thought Demarcus would lead him to your father.

Tatum looked up. "To kill him."

"Yes," Nuieve said.

"Why?"

"Because your grandfather was also searching for him to take his place as Chief until you became of age. The child Motif created with Ky would leave with him back to his home land.....unless something happens to the firstborn.

"Motif been on this island under false pretense from the beginning. His mother was the concubine of his father Chief De'amdre.' The chief's wife was never able to reproduce. When Vilmander found out, it was too late. His only hope was his grandson, who's fathered by another man. As Ky requested, Demarcus kept you close by his side after her death. Whatever tutor Motif tried to hired, Demarcus had them thrown off the island into exile. Motif went in front of Council more times than I can count, complaining about how *his* son was being handle. But Demarcus stayed four steps ahead. Plus, Motif didn't plan on you being gifted." He smiled to himself. "By the time he found out you finished high school, I thinkyou were picking members of your pack. Anyway, when his plan fell through, because

Demarcus couldn't lead him to your father, he needed another plan. Anything to keep him on this island. So he blackmailed me after walking in on us."

"How could you let something like that happen?" Do I really want to understand is the real question."

"Vilmander had died and Cassandra stayed on after the birth of Moham, even though Gerox cut all ties with us, she was still hoping to get a glimpse of him, before we marry and move to her island. We only had two weeks before we became man and wife, but Motif was desperate. When Demarcus took you, Ky, and Cole on a get-a-way to take your mind off things, that's when he had me. I was trapped by Motif and there was no way out. My life with Cassandra would never happen as long as he stayed Chief."

"I'm sorry Nuieve, but as I sit here as Chief now, I can't grant you that. The best I can do is petition against Council to let you retire early. Maybe send you somewhere as far away from Motif as possible. But exiling Motif from this island is going to take some time, because he's been ruler too long."

"Not if we prove to the people that the former Chief bloodline is not leading this land. Motif has force people from their lands and homes claiming he's Chief. Everything he did will be void. He will leave with what he came with."

"But to do that, we'll have to find my biological father. These people don't believe in scientific testing and I don't know if he will be open minded to go through our traditional way. And no offense, but I have too much shit here to do, than go hunting around the world right now. Which reminds me, we need to make that announcement. Can you get Council together early in the morning? I don't know how, but you'll have to do it without giving them an explanation *and* Motif have to be there."

For some reason, I'm getting a suffocating feeling that Jameria is way more important than what we're expecting. "Who has the information for our Mistress," I said, interrupting the back and forward squabble between him and Tatum.

They stopped in the middle of talking and stared at me. "As our Chief said, the Mistress is not here. Her situation is delicate. So if it's important, we have to get it for her."

Nuieve was already shaking his head no. "Ky said Jameria eyes only."

"Why didn't you give it to her years ago Nuieve? Hell, you could've gave it to her as a wedding gift for all I cared. But why so long?" Tyvine still had a hard time grasping it. I wasn't hanging on tight myself.

"I tried so many times. But being blackmailed by Motif as he robbed us, our neighboring friends, our people......So many people watching. He has eyes everywhere. Look, Motif and a few of his friends left yesterday morning for the mainland. If I knew when he'll be back, I could call the meeting as soon as he get off the boat."

"Call the meeting. I'll make sure he comes back."

Nuieve stared at him. "Will Jameria go through the 'Birthing Ritual?'"

Tatum looked at Nuieve, pulled his cloak over his head before walking out of the sitting room door.

Once the night air hit us, the tension eased. We stood side by side, staring up at the full moon. Simultaneously, we discarded our cloaks. Exhilarating in the cool earth beneath our feet. Balloon black britches caressing my muscled thighs as the wind tried to take us on another journey. We released the rubber bands from our hair, letting it flow on the strong breeze coming from the east. We took off in a hard run, heading straight for the woods. Leaping over fallen trees, broken branches stabbing in our feet, bushes and tree limbs whipping across our bodies. Yet, we ran faster.

Through my peripheral vision, wolves in our flank was running just as hard. Soon we were surrounded, still keeping pace.

We slowed when the opening came into view. Then a complete stop right in front of the alpha wolf and his mate.

Two beautiful pups were sitting on their cute little paws in from of their parents. The alpha wolf butt their little rears with his snout, urging them forward. Tatum got on one knee, opening his arms accepting them. He lifted both pups in his arms, cradling them like babies. They immediately started yelping and licking his face. Tatum stood. The alpha wolf and his mate bowed to him before turning and entering the woods. We stood there until every single wolf disappeared from our sight. We turned, making our own slow journey back to the palace.

Tyvine got closer beside him, pulling a pup from his arm. "What are you going to name them?"

The pup that remained in his arm was chewing on the hand woven bracelet circling his wrist. He started laughing to himself. "Hey, do you remember those two old drunks that wondered onto Jameria's private road at the farm house?"

I smiled, reminiscing. "Yeah, they was looking for the old woman who sold the moonshine. Jameria had to mix something up just to get them away from the house."

"Or at least off the porch. They was so funky, Kelanie had dozens of birds flapping their wings to fan the air around them," Tyvine said laughing. "We had a name for them......"

"Chewy and Louie," Tatum said, still looking at the little fur ball that was gnawing away.

We went to Tatum's chambers, no longer hiding. All we needed was one person to see us then Motif will be on his way back home.

Chapter 15

Pierce.............

I don't believe it.....and I defiantly didn't want to hear it. My father was near panic mode. His life might be in danger, because Nuieve decided to involve him in something he's not ready for.

"Where's Motif now?"

My father sat, drinking his cognac straight from the bottle. "Last I heard, him and some of his rowdy friends took his boat to the mainland."

No one is supposed to know Jameria is back on the island, but......

"Don't fret yourself, son. All I have to do is wait a little while longer, then whatever is in the box will be in the Mistress hands as soon as she gets back."

Tatum is going to kill me.

I went to dad's private closet, removing the black cloak from the hanger.

When I returned to the sitting room and he saw what was in my hand, he swallowed the last of his drink stored in his mouth. "What's that for?"

"Here. Put it on," I said, tossing it to him. I hope the Mistress understand what I'm doing. I love my father too much to let him be mixed up in this. So I need to get this burden off of him tonight. "Come with me."

I led him out of his corridor vault door, heading straight for the forest. I didn't bother to look up at the moon. The maca root Jameria put in our food, helped us find our true instinct. In the bayou, we did a lot of poling, fishing and deer hunting. It was a simple life. One I could actually get used to.

Once the jungle swallowed us from the palace lights, I told my dad to stay close, because one mistake and he'll never be heard from again.

"Where are we going, Pierce?"

I could tell he was nervous. My father has never been a part of a pack. Like Demarcus, he started his training early as an elder, taking over the set of my grandfather.

"I don't want Motif or anyone harming you. I know that box is the biggest problem in your life right now. I hate Nuieve involved you in this."

He grabbed my shoulder, bringing me to a halt. "I would die for Jameria a million times over, if I had to. Whatever I can do to help her I will." If he only knew the value of that box, he'd know that more than his life is in danger.

We walked on until Jade's emerald green eyes lit the path to our destination. Marlease paused when he saw the huge anaconda.

"Just keep walking dad. As long as you're with me, everything is going to be fine." *I hope.*

We walked directly ahead, passing Jade and into the land of snakes. Snakes of all shapes and sizes, hanging from trees, bathing in the moonlight on rocks, mating in the grass, or slithering in dozens toward the shallow pit.

"My God," Marlease said, practically shaking in his shoes.

I kept encouraging him until we made it to the edge of the pit. Marelease gasped when he saw Jameria smack in the center of the pit, asleep in her white silk pajamas with a long white flowing silk robe over them. Snakes slithered across her balloon belly and through her long wavy hair.

"Is she alright?"

I laughed softly. "She's perfectly safe."

Tatum and Jameria spent many nights in this pit just to keep the snakes away during the first few months of her pregnancy.

A black gaboon slithered in front of me. I quickly pick it up by its head. I bit into my forearm until it bled, letting a few drops land on the snake's fangs. Then I threw it into the pit close to where Jameria lay. Her eyes snapped open immediately, searching until they collided with mine. She saw the desperation and the fear mingling on the brink of insanity in my father's eyes. She let out a sharp hiss, calling to those in the distance as well. My father watched in amazement as the snakes lifted our

Mistress up and out of the pit to us. I grabbed her hands pulling her into my arms.

She held my tall frame close. "What's wrong, Pierce," she said against my chest. "Why would you bring your father to such a place?"

I pulled back, looking deep into her eyes. "I'm sorry Mistress, but there's something my father must tell you."

She turned to Marlease and for a moment he was too frighten to say anything. Jameria smiled at him, eased herself out of my arms and went to take his hand. "It's okay, Elder Marlease. You can tell me anything."

Marelase dropped his head as his shoulders began to shake with his sobs.

"Just start from the beginning," she sooth.

As my dad filled Jameria in on his conversation with Nuieve, I saw his shoulders pull back and stand a little bit straighter, like a huge weight had been lifted.

"Do you have the information with you," she asked.

"No," he said, already shaking his head from side to side. "Pierce never said where we were going, so I didn't think it was necessary to bring it."

She thought a moment. "Pierce go with your father and bring that package to me. Elder Marlease, I wish I can send you away from this place right now, but in a few hours a meeting will be called and you *have* to be there to witness."

"Send me away?" He was surprised.

"At least for a little while. The one thing I don't want, is for Motif to find out you're helping us. I hope you understand."

Marlease bowed his head again. "Of course."

We turned to leave.

"Pierce?"

I turned back.

"Don't go to the others. Come straight here…..as fast as you can."

When we made it back to his suite, I disrobe my cloak leaving it in the middle of the floor. He went to his bed room to retrieve the box he put the information in. I went to his storage closet to retrieve a backpack. Once I joined Marlease in the sitting room, I saw he had several other items on the coffee table surrounding a box covered in bronze silk material with the initials JB sewn into the fabric.

"I gathered some supplies for you and the Mistress. From what Nuieve told me, I'm guessing there will be some hiking."

Thinking fast, I ran down the hall to Jameria's personal room to retrieve her hiking boots. My father had everything packed and ready to go. I placed her boots in a satchel and tied it across my bare chest.

Marlease came to me and embraced me in a bear hug. "Be careful. I don't know what I'll do if anything happens to you."

I looked directly into eyes like mine. Standing at his six foot two inch height, I placed my hand on his shoulder. "I'll be fine. Just don't worry yourself to death. Make reservations for a short trip. You need a vacation," I said looking at him pointedly.

Once I was back outside of the palace, my first instinct was to look up at the full moon. The wind blew taking strains of my hair east. I let my animal instinct take over my body like Tatum taught me. With adrenaline pumping in my veins, I took off at top speed, running like my life depended on it. Fallen tree branches jabbing me in my feet. Wild limbs whipping me as I pass.

It only took a few minutes to make it back to the Mistress. She had a back pack of her own on her left shoulder. I slowed to a trout then walked the rest of the way to her, removing the satchel from across my chest.

"Here. I brought you some durable shoes." She didn't argue the fact that I was going with her. I guess she figured when neither of us returned to the palace, our family won't be too worried......at least I hope.

I took the box from the backpack, placing it on a sturdy boulder. Jameria just stared at it.

"And Tatum's mother left this for me?"

I hunched my shoulders. "That's what dad said."

She took her short knife that she always keep strap to her inner thigh and slid it across the top of the cardboard box. She took out the silk wrapped box, running her fingers across her initials. She then removed the box from the silk shelter, holding it up in the moonlight. The box itself had priceless emeralds and diamonds set in an elaborate design. But it was the lock that drew your attention. It was obvious that a key did not fit.

Jameria looked at it closely before her eyes bucked in surprise. Then she removed the diamond belly chain she use to wear around her waist, from around her neck. Tatum had Demarcus buy her that chain as a welcoming gift. But from the way Jameria's studying it, it might be more precious than she thought. When she finally made it to the diamond she was looking for, she inserted it into the lock and the box popped open. Inside the box were several documents in a Ziploc bag, private diaries, and a single key. Jameria shifted through the documents until she landed on one addressed to her.

We both looked at each other in surprise. I couldn't help myself.

I looked over her shoulder as she read the letter to herself.

Hello Jameria,

I know this may come as a surprise to you, but I've wanted

To meet you since the day you entered this world. Let me explain myself. You see Jameria, I am a weak woman when it comes to my children. Which is why this letter is addressed to you. I'm going to ask you to do something that will change the course of events in your life, but if you're not strong enough a lot of people will suffer. All of that depends on you.

The day I found out I was pregnant with my first born was the same day I took my marriage vows with Motif. I knew immediately the child wasn't his, because the only man I've ever lain with was my one and only true love, Dominique. I kept this secret from Motif for as long as I could. And the closer I was to give birth to Tatum, the more stressed I was about the 'Birthing Ritual.'

Then one day I received a letter in the mail from a lady named Patricia Ann Beau. Your grandmother. In the letter she told me about a visit she received from   a   young handsome man who was desperately trying to save my life. He told her that he needed help to save me from a sick art that was practice before the beginning of time. Your grandmother decided to help him and believe me, she did.

But it came at a high price. As desperate as Dominique was trying to save me, Pat Ann was going through her own drama. Her daughter was about to give birth to you. She didn't want to take away your freedom, but she also didn't want you to live the type of life your mother lives. She wanted you to be safe.

So a plan was made.

The plan was after the birth of the two children, they would be linked by blood. Your closeness to my son is no coincidence. Pat Ann linked you two through your fathers to make sure you found each other. To you it might sound like a voodoo curse, but it was the only way we could save both of our children.

As promised, your grandmother saved my life. The 'Birthing Ritual' would have surely killed me. What you need is buried in your engagement ring, the cave I made Tatum promise to give his future wife. I'm sorry to put such a burden on your young shoulders, but as I sit writing this letter, Motif's fetus is growing stronger in my womb. A child that should've never been created. A child that will destroy you and Tatum both. As a mother I cannot kill my own. And Tatum is sensitive when it comes to anyone who's a part of me. You will have to do what my son and I cannot. You will have to end Motif's bloodline before he ends Tatum's. You have to kill my second born son.

You probably think he can be saved, but this is not so. Motif's already making plans for his son. He didn't include Tatum in those plans, other than to marry him off of this island. But if you're reading this letter, then the blessings are in my favor. Please take care of Tatum. Protect his Pack.

KY

Jameria folded the letter and placed it back in the box, slamming I shut before she removed the diamond link chain from the lock.

We stared at each other.

"Wow," I said.

"Yeah," she replied.

What else could be said?

We both started moving, immediately. I put the box back in my backpack while she slipped on jogging pants over her pajama pants. When she slipped her feet in her boots, I bent down to tie them for her.

"I look ridiculous," she said, placing her backpack on her shoulder.

I stood looking her up and down. Her long wavy black hair was in a messy bun on top of her head. The jogging pants and hiking boots was fine, but her swollen breast and huge belly stood out like a sore thumb.

"Stop looking at me like that," she snapped. I couldn't help myself. For the first time, the 'bronze beauty,' looks like an ordinary person.

It was three in the morning when we finally made it to the caves. Jameria had brought along two snakes, to dissolve my worries. Once we entered the cave known as her engagement ring, it took my breath away. The cave was wide and spacious. Diamonds imbedded in the rocks made the dome cave ceiling sparkle like star at night. The ground floor was smooth like velvet. There was a king size bed set directly in the middle of the cave with bronze and white silk sheets. Two of Jameria's humongous snakes lay guarding the precious rocks. One of the snakes was so familiar to me.......like the back of my hand.

"Coral? Is that Coral," I said instinctively moving towards him. AS soon as I said his name, the six and half long *micrurus tener* glided to me, wrapping around my ankles and slithered up my body. His lisp tongue tapped my cheek three times.

I couldn't stop the tears from drenching my face. I let my hand glide across his scales, not believing what I was seeing......feeling. Jameria kissed his head as we embraced.

"How long?" I could utter no more words.

"As soon as I found out I was pregnant."

"Why didn't you tell us?" I was beyond hurt the Mistress would keep something like this from us.

"Because I didn't want you to hate me after he left again. This is only temporary," she said as her fingers glided down his scaled body.

"Carmen would love to have met you."

"I'm sorry, Pierce. Please don't tell the others. Losing Coral once was hard enough for the Pack."

I understood completely.

Jameria removed the box from my backpack again, unlocked it, and took out the map that was hand drawn by Tatum's mother herself. Then she took out a bottle of water and a small shovel. Walked at least 29 to 30 centimeters coming upon a large boulder that is now used as a table for her lamp and a picture of her and Tatum in a diamond frame.

She dug around the boulder for a while until she pulled up a tarnish gold locket. After looking at it for a long time, she put the locket aside and dug in that spot until her shovel hit something metal. I went and pick up the locket, curious. Inside was baby pictures of Tatum on one side and the Mistress on the other. Jameria's grandmother must've sent her picture to Ky.

I released Coral from my embrace. Knowing how the Mistress hates to be helped, I knelt beside her, in front of the boulder and started digging right along with her, not waiting for permission. I pulled the metal box out of its resting place, laying it in front of her to open. She released the latch, lifted the lid and inside on top of a chocolate brown pillow was a small bottle and a little note:

I've already used half Jameria. You use the other half. Your

grandmother sent this to me a couple of months before Tatum was born. Only you, Tatum, the Council and a servant, will be present during the ritual. Other family members can be invited, but I strongly suggest to keep it closed. The Council and the Chief will have a celebration drink while you are in labor. This is very important: Make sure your chosen servant is someone you can trust. I cannot stress that enough. Whoever you choose will be the one to mix the traditional drinks. I pray this works in your favor. Take care of my son and grandchild.   Ky

Jameria held up the bottle looking at the contents inside. Then pass the bottle to me. "You're going to be at that ritual as my servant. And this will never be mentioned again."

Chapter 16

Tyvine.............

"What do you mean they haven't returned yet?! Did anyone check with Marlease?" Tatum was about to commit a murder.

 The Mistress and our pack brother has been out all night, Motif's yacht has been spotted entering the dock, and we don't know if Nuieve got everyone together for the announcement.

"Where the fuck is my wife?! Why hasn't she returned yet?"

 At those words Pierce walked through the door with Jameria right behind him.

"Where in the hell have you two been," Tatum said pulling his mate to him for a tight embrace.

I watched as Pierce and Jameria traded looks. Pierce went to Carmen for a quick kiss. Nothing was said. He just stared into his mates eyes, as if that was all the communication they needed.

"Never mind. You're here now," Tatum continued. "This is only a short visit. We had to tell you of some important information one of the elders have for you."

 Again, the strange look between Pierce and our Mistress.

"Nuieve told us my mom left something here-"

"We know."

"What?"

Jameria spoke louder. "We know. And please don't question us. This is not something we can speak on. Trust me." She looked at Pierce. "Trust us."

Tatum stared into his mate's eyes, then he looked at his youngest pack brother. Standing at six foot and a couple of inches all muscled lean body, our youngest brother Pierce, had to do therapy. Boaz and Shy did a number on him and Carmen. To the point that if Carmen didn't come forward when she did, Boaz would've passed her around to every leading man he knew. When Tatum was told in detail about Boaz rampage, he knew there was no turning back for his little brother. All because he wanted the title.

Scratch that.

All because he wanted Jameria. His brother's wife.

"Okay," Tatum said. "No more questions. We have to go. Motif's boat should've docked by now. We just came back to give you the info we got from Nuieve." He kissed his wife, before he turned to leave.

"Wait. You have to take Pierce with you."

He turned back to her confused now. "For what?"

"Pierce have to be at the ritual as my servant."

We *all* turned to look at her confused.

"I thought Rubae` was going to be the servant to help deliver the baby. I didn't know Pierce was skilled in child birth.......I don't understand."

I looked at Pierce. His expression was blank, but I could easily see the determination in the way he stood with his back straight, chest out, and head held high. He didn't say a word. Just kissed his mates lips quickly and left out of the door.

"Do Pierce know how to deliver a baby," I asked.

The Mistress smiled for the first time after walking back into her adoptive father's suite. "Don't worry. I'll have him ready."

That was good enough or me. If she says she's going to have him ready, then he will *be* ready.

I pulled Cougar up off the sofa, circling her in my arms. Her belly wasn't big, but I still felt a distance away. Pregnant or not, my Cougar is a hellcat. If she *think* something is wrong, jaguars, lions, or maybe even panthers will tear through this place like a Louisiana hurricane. "Please be patient, baby. If you don't hear from us that means you just need to be a little more patient."

She poked her lip out, then planed a quick kiss on me. "Fine. But remember you bought us cell phones. Use them." She walked off to Jameria's room.

After Karden and Kelanie's long kiss goodbye the four of us made our way to the Council Hall. Long gasps of surprise and happy citizens greeted and bowed to their new Chief. Murmurs of wonder about their Mistress' location. And gossip already circling about why she's not by his side.

We entered the hall in a single line. Then stood side by side in the center of the floor. The council members were shocked to see us. Even Nuieve had a look of surprise on his face. God only knows what he told them to get them to agree to this meeting.

Elder Marlease came to the podium. "Gentlemen. This is a pleasant surprise. If we'd known about the Pack's return, your people would've greeted you more properly, other than surprised glances."

Understanding washed over us like a relieving painkiller. All the secrecy between Jameria and Pierce was clear once we looked into the young elder's eyes. They were protecting him.

Tatum stepped forward. "We came to make an announcement, sir. But due to the fact that my uncle and our mates with a couple of our brothers could not be in attendance today, we will also have to represent for them."

"And why is that?" Elder Nuieve was playing his part well. I wonder what the panel would think of him if they found out he gets off my sucking dick.

"Our mates. Jameria in particular, is six months pregnant."

The uproar came from the entrance of the meeting hall. Motif, Noonie, his right-hand man Remy, and pack brother Boris stood in the doorway staring at us as if we were ghost. Motif came through the door, marching pass outstretched hands, trying to stop him. I grabbed the right just as Karen grabbed the left of Tatum's arms. Going for Motif's throat has become the norm for our Chief. Before Motif took another step, I leaned into my protective crouch in front of Tatum. Out of my peripheral, I saw Pierce take my flank. Remy rushed forward, passing Motif coming right for me. Pierce moved like a flash of lightning, tagging Remy's body with a series of upper-cuts, elbows, knee thrusts. Martial art combos that took Remy to the ground within seconds.

Motif was upon us now. I rushed him, close-hanging his ass like Tatum did at the first announcement meeting. It took Karden to pull me off of him. I tried to put his ass back in the infirmary.....or worse.

"It's not for you to end his life Ty," Karden whispered in my ear.

I looked up in time to see Boris heading for Pierce and Remy.

Tatum, our Chief, our friend, our leading pack brother, barked a call that made the ground rumble beneath our feet.

Everyone paused.

Then.......

We heard them running. Soon the meeting hall was filled with wolves. I stood backing up, pulling Karden with me whose eyes were glued to the unbelievable show before us.

Tatum received his gift.

When? That's the part I'm still trying to figure out.

As soon as the thought came, something within me bubbled up and left my lips. It was a deep growl. Before I knew it I was in a crouch again. Red clouded my vision. I poised to attack, waiting on my pack leader to bark the call. I salved from my mouth at the thought of tasting my prey's blood. I was no longer defending. I wanted to kill. Next to me, I heard my brother's deep breathing. A growl ripped from his lips. He stared at our prey like fresh meat. Pierce stood from the man who was as still as a board on the floor. His body lying in a pool of blood.

Motif and his men were surrounded by at least three dozen wolves.

"Tatum," Nuieve yelled. "Tatum, please. This is not how you want this to end. Don't condemn your life or the lives of your brothers like this."

The next bark from Tatum cleared my head. I was myself again. Soon the room was clear. Right at the entry of the door, I saw two cloaked figures recede back into the shadows. No doubt Cole and Moham heard the call as well.

What the fuck is going on?!

"I can't do this," Boris said. "I didn't sign up or this Motif." He looked at Tatum. "I didn't come to do you any harm. I want to exile myself from this island. I don't know who or what you are. Whatever you and Motif got going on, I want no part of it. I just want to leave in peace……Please."

"You are a part of *my* pack. I could have your head for your so called loyalty." Motif's anger was now pointed at his pack brother.

"He's your son, Motif. Do you hate him so much that you're willing to die for a title that he's been groomed for, anyway?"

Motif went for his neck. But Boris was quick. He took Motif's legs from under him in one swift motion.

"You're no longer chief. You're not even an elder. My life is not tied to you anymore. Stay the fuck away from me." He looked to Tatum again. "Can me and my family please leave?"

Tatum granted his wish and Boris left without even a glance back.

"Is Remy alive," Elder Mara asked. It still amazed me that Mara is actually Karden's father.

They have *nothing* common.

Mara is an elder that belong in the bitch category. If Motif threw a bone and told him to jump, he wouldn't question how high before he skipped his punk ass in the air. Elder or not, I'll fuck his ass up if he's even thinking about fucking with Pierce. Whether they know or not, my brothers and I were blooded one way or the other. What Pierce did was no different from what the rest of us did.

We just didn't do it in front of an audience.

Motif kept his eye on Karden as he checked for a pulse on Remy.

"He's still breathing. Just unconscious."

Tatum looked at our youngest pack brother with proud eyes. "Are you alright?"

"Are you fucking serious?! He nearly beat the man to death. He needs to be put in a cage like that beast of a bitch you call a wife! Noonie's face still haven't healed and that attack was months ago!"

"We will handle this Motif," Mara said, staring daggers at Nuieve. He knew this was a set-up. "Pierce must be punished for his reckless and abusive behavior."

Karden turned to his father, his back now facing Motif. "Did you not see Remy charging at Tyvine?"

"Don't Karden. I don't want to fight with you, again. Your pack might be the new leaders, but all of you are way out of control."

"No," Marlease said.

"I'm sorry, Elder Marlease, but if we don't discipline him-"

"You mean break him?" Tatum turned to face the panel, his back now to Motif, too. I moved to stand directly behind Tatum, facing Motif. "Did Motif tell you Boaz is no longer a part of our pack?" Shocked gasps vibrated through the hall. "Did he tell you he had his youngest son and mate force his pack brother and sister to do vile and unimaginable things, I can't bring myself to say aloud. Why should Pierce be punished when the former Chief forced my hand so many times? And will Boaz be punished for his crimes, Elder Mara? He and Shyamae` disobeyed my orders as their Chief many times over."

"I'm sorry, Tatum, We have no record-"

"I filed each complaint and dated them, father. If you would check with your officials, they will give you all of the necessary documents. Boaz has been running wild for some time now. All because our former Chief promised him the title of this land. A title that is in Tatum's right. As Motif's first born son, it is in his right to be Chief. Yet, now that he *is* Chief, you're finding ways to punish us when it's Motif and his pack members who attack first," Karden said. He'd taken several steps toward the podium without noticing, with his hands clenched into fists. He glared at his father with such disgust, I thought Karden was gonna pounce.

Motif walked around us in a large arch. "I want to see these false records. These allegations against my son-"

"Which one Motif?" It was my father speaking this time. Elder Gramz.

 My father and I lived the normal life before I became a pack member. Standing at six foot seven inches, my father is a formidable man. He never hassled me or meddled in my business. He raised me like any bachelor raising a son. Hired nurses and tutors was my part time mothers. Once I joined the pack at the age of thirteen, his fathering days was over.

"Which one what," Motif said, stopping in his tracks. He never had a run in with my father. His size and weight, who would?

But to Jameria and Cougar, my father is like a flirtatious cuddly bear and will forever be my beautiful mate's champion. Whatever Cougar wants, Cougar gets if my father have to say anything about it.

"Which one of your sons are you defending? Because it seems to me you're not even claiming Tatum. Why do you want your second born to be named Chief and not the one who was groom for this position?"

Silence.

Everyone was so quiet, you could hear a pin drop.

Motif looked at everyone on the panel. Then he turned and looked at Tatum. Tatum smiled at him.

He knew.

He know that Tatum knows about his parentage.

"It's not like that," he said turning back to the panel. "I just see a better future for this land if Boaz succeeded me. We have to set an example for our people, and the things Tatum and his pack is doing, is just unnatural. Boaz is more sensitive. He doesn't use barbaric gestures and attack his father in public. And now they've created spawns." Motif looked back at Tatum. "And although the young Mistress is with child, I also heard our new Chief say she is now SIX MONTHS PREGNANT?! Young Chief, you was only gone 3 to 4 months. Sounds like to me, she was already a couple of months along before the wedding."

Tatum smiled, his long hair cascading around his body like a shield. Staring at the man like a roach beneath the sole of his shoe. "I thought a woman's cycle is her business, but of course if I have to explain about a regular cycle and an irregular cycle, would be quite embarrassing. Other than that, it was normal for our mates to miss a cycle or two. They're very active women."

"That's because you let them run wild-"

"Enough Motif," my father said with a raised hand. "I want to get back to the subject of ruler. You challenged your first born right here in this room, in our witness. I think I speak for the rest of the Elders when I say, something fishy is going on. Now once we review the records of complaint they've left with Kilmya, then we'll regroup. But we do have a few questions of our own. The first is, where's Boaz," Elder Gramz asked, looking between Motif and Tatum.

"I have no idea Elder," Tatum said hunching his shoulders. "Once we exposed him of his treachery, him and his mate left and went their own way the day of the wedding."

"So it's true. He's disband from your pack, Motif whispered under his breath. Then aloud he said, "Elder, Boaz will be here at the end of the month." He was up to something. Now he looked as if he wanted to break out in a jig.

"So you know where Boaz is," Nuieve asked.

"Yes, he said looking up at the panel. "As I said, Boaz show respect to his people. It wasn't treachery towards his brothers. It was respect for his country. Demonstrating violence in crowds is not Boaz," he said. Then he turned, walking out of the door with the guards carrying Remy's body to the infirmary. He smiled gleefully at Tatum like he'd won the war.

Elder Gramz looked at Tatum. "Young Chief, what was that with the wolves? It seems at a sporadic moment of anger, you and your pack brothers-"

"Please," I said looking at my father. "That is one question my Chief or mybrothers and I cannot answer at this time. Not only was it sporadic, but it's also the first time something like that has ever happened." I looked at each and every one of them, on the panel. "Please let us figure it out first."

"Very well," Mara said. "Bu as Motif has pointed out, these acts of violence your pack is demonstrating will be examined as well as your allegations against your pack brother and former Chief."

Gramz continued. "When will your wives return?"

"They will be here in a few weeks with Elder Demarcus. We just wanted to rush back to make the official announcement."

"This is wonderful news. Karden, Tyvine, congratulations to you both as well. But young Pierce, this is not-"

"No Elder," Tatum said, waving his hands. "Young Carmen is not with child. Pierce will be representing the Mistress as her servant."

That damn look of surprise again.

"Pierce," Nuieve whispered.

"Pierce," my father said, just as surprised. "Pierce is going to deliver your baby?"

"Yes," Tatum said with his head held high. "It's both mine and the Mistress wishes."

"Well Pierce," Marlease said. "I never knew you were studying to be a doctor."

Huh. That's not a bad idea for our little brother. All the pussy Boaz had him buried in, will make him a great gynecologist.

Pierce just smiled up at his father.

"Young Tatum, will young Boaz remain as your wife left-hand man or has that too changed?"

Tatum was already walking to the podium with his note. "Yes sir. I decided to go with another person. Someone I should've picked at first," he said handing Gramz the paper."

Gramz looked at the paper, bouncing his head up and down. "I agree. He will be equipped with the necessary training. If there is nothing else, you gentlemen are excused until further notice. And please stay out of Motif's way. He is our former Chief who ran this land for the past eighteen years. Just show a little respect," he said looking at me winking. He turned and left the podium, followed by the rest of the elders.

My brothers and I walked out of the meeting hall into the courtyard. Loyal citizens bowed or greeted us as we passed.

We went straight for the north wing. No doubt eyes were watching us everywhere.

As soon as we entered the Mistress suite, I headed to the bathroom to retrieve the cell phones we stashed earlier. I tossed Tatum and Karden theirs and laid Pierce's on the counter. He went to take a shower to remove all the blood dried on his skin and glued in his hair. I went in the bedroom for some privacy, giving Cougar every play by play moment.

"Baby, it was unreal. What Tatum did was no different from what you, Jameria or any of our other sisters can do. The only difference was *we* was under his control too."

"I know. Cole and Moham was sitting with Tyce and Maria when all of a sudden they was tossing on their cloaks, sprinting out of the door," she said.

"What is Jameria's take on this?"

Silence.

"I'll let Tatum explain it to you guys. Jameria's on the phone explaining it to him now."

"Cougar, did Jameria do something to us?"

The long pause again.

"Cougar?"

"She did it for us, love. It was the only way we knew you guys and our children would be safe if anything happened to us."

I was already walking to the door. I saw Karden in the library den with his own phone at his ear, heading in the same direction. Tatum's back was to us.

"We'll talk about this later," I said before hanging up.

Karden hung his up, too.

We waited.

When he hung up, he turned with a look of astonishment written all over his face. "She linked us by blood. That's why she wanted to go back to her farmhouse....Pat Ann's house. Her *traiteur* grandmother," he said shaking his bowed head.

"They asked her to do it," Karden said, death in his voice. "They thought if anything happened to them-," he broke off. He just couldn't say it.

Pierce walked out of the bathroom. It only took him a second to catch the vibe in the room. "What's happened now," he said sighing.

"Pierce, what happen to you and Jameria? Where did you go," Tatum asked.

Pierce stared a Tatum with blank eyes, as if he was in a battle within himself.

Tatum waited patiently for the boys answer.

Pierce dropped his head. "I can't tell you that Chief Tatum. I *cannot* break my word to her. Jameria's trust in me at this point is valuable to her life. I'm sorry. I cannot say."

Tatum smiled. "I respect you for that, Pierce. Please forgive *me* this time for trying to force your hand."

Then Pierce looked up with a devilish smile of his own. "Just don't drink the tea." Then he turned and went back in the bathroom.

 We all stared in confusion, wondering what the hell did that mean.

Chapter 17

Moham.........

My tongue dove deep, so deep I tried to touch her womb. My hand jerked at a rapid speed, pulling hard on my dick. No doubt mirroring my brothers.

What the fuck did I let this woman do to me?"

Her soft moans had my dick head swelling to unimaginable proportions. Her feminine scent had me digging deeper into her womanhood. Then my son kicked the shit out of her where I rested my hand on her swollen belly. His way of letting me know I won't be sticking my pole in her tonight.

Dammit.

I climbed up on the bed, my hand still working my member. I aimed it at Tyce's beautiful pale face.

"Sorry baby," I said before I shoved my length in her mouth.

When I came, it hit me like a spasm. My nut still flowing as I stared up at the full moon.

The sick part about this whole thing is my brothers busted the same nut whether they was jacking off or with their mates. And since Tatum, Tyvine, and Karden was on the other side of the palace while their mates slept peacefully in the next room, it was obvious their hands kept them company tonight.

Tyce got up and went to the bathroom. I laid flat on my back with my forearm covering my eyes. Jameria's confession was haunting me to no end.

She linked us.

Something her grandmother taught her a long time ago and also told her to never speak of. But Jameria loved her sisters...and her sisters love her.

The entire three months we was on the farm, they'd been feeding us 'maca root.' An herbal root from the ancient Pumpush tribe. Part of Jameria's ancestral heritage.

They thought they was going to die. And even after death, they would try to find a way to keep us safe.

My Tyce apologized many times over. She didn't have to.

I didn't want her to.

Then there's the Mistress.

She'd been in deep thought since she returned with Pierce a few days ago. Though she kept her face blank, I know her well enough to know when she's stressing about something. And that's defiantly not good in her condition.

I need to see her.

I got up and went to the vanity room. Tyce was still soaking in her bubble bath. I took a quick shower, dried off, and slipped on my black pajama pants. Then I went to my wife and kissed her lightly on the lips.

"Don't stay in too long. I'll be back soon." She smiled at me with sleepy eyes before they closed again. "Get out of the tub," I said more firmly. I reached between her legs and pulled up the stopper.

This isn't the first time I caught her like this. But the tubs in the States were much safer than the ones here in the palace. These are too deep. Once I made sure Tyce was tucked safely in bed, I went to the Mistress's suite. I entered her sitting room and knocked on her bedroom door.

"Come in."

I entered her room to find her sitting in her desk chair by the window facing the moon. Her wavy black hair flowed around her shoulders like a shawl. Her long white gown doing nothing to hide her huge middle. I don't think she can get any bigger without doubling over. She looked at me and smiled. Her even white teeth against her bronze skin lighting up the room as well as my spirits. I went to her falling on my knees, throwing my arms around her hips and burying my face in her lap.

"Oh Mo," she said running her fingers through my hair. She let me cry until my tears ran dry.

My only secret I kept from everyone, but Jameria.

Before Jameria, it was Tatum's mother, Ky. In between, I just cried myself to sleep. It don't happen often, only when it feels like I'm too stressed on my anxiety attacks kick in. I thought me having a mate like Tatum's was the cure and for a while it worked. I thought I could do anything as long as I have Tyce. But the thought of losing her, had me falling back into that same routine.

Once I was through with my last sniffle, she stood, pulling me up with her. She sat on the edge of her bed and put two pillows on the floor between her legs, gesturing for me to have a seat. I grabbed the brush off her vanity table and got comfortable on the floor. She took long slow strokes. We didn't speak. Just enjoyed the quiet moment with my head resting on her inner thigh and her brushing my hair. This is what I love about the Mistress. She's easy to talk to. Always let you move at your own pace.

She continued brushing

After a moment I asked, "What if you *do* make it?"

Her hand paused in the middle of a stroke. Then she continued. "You worry too much."

I smiled. "Are you being the pot or the skillet this time," I said, referring to a folktale she always repeat about a pot calling a skillet black.

She laughed. "Touché."

"You know Tatum is going to kill everybody on this island if anything happens to you. I don't know what you and Pierce have planned, but I suggest you include our Chief. Leaving him out of *this* loophole might be too dangerous."

Her hand stilled.

"I'm sorry, Mistress. I should mind my own bus-"

"We're family," she said, leaning down, hugging my neck. "And you're right. Tatum needs to be included, but I was given specific instructions. Yet, I can't let Pierce do this all by himself. I've been puzzling my mind about this all day."

I patted her arm. Smooth her hair back over her shoulder. "We all come to you with our problems. Who do you have to go to with yours?"

She laughed. "Well, my dad actually. But as you can see, his absence is taking its toll on me."

"Ahhh. You miss your daddy," I said mocking her.

She laughed, hitting me with a pillow.

"Hey Jameria," Cole said, walking in without announcing himself, as usual. He climbed up on the bed and grabbed the remote, flipping through channels. "When is dad coming home? He's laid up in Rubae' long enough. Call the man and tell him to put some draws on and get back here. You're about to pop and he's freaking your nurse on the other side of the world." Jameria was already on her phone, texting.

"Don't text him. Call the man. Hell, he needs to hear the phone ring."

"I'm texting Pierce."

"For what? Demarcus listens to you. Not Pierce."

"No, Cole. I'm telling him, I decided to include one more person in our plans for the 'Birthing Ritual,'" she said looking at me with a smile, like I was a conspirator in a secret that really only included her and Pierce.

I was about to go back to my room until the next visitor surprised us with a soft knock.

"Oh, it must be Maria. That girl just can't get enough of this."

Jameria sighed, rolling her eyes.

Laughing, I went to the door to let her in. "See you guys in the morning, I said, thinking I was about to leave."

I opened the door and thought my eyes was deceiving me. I blinked several times, praying I wasn't seeing things.

"What's wrong," Jameria asked.

I stepped aside.

Demarcus, Rubae' and Jameria's biological mother and father entered the room. On instinct, I closed and locked the door. Cole and Jameria sat on the bed staring at but one individual. Then they both jumped up running into Demarcus' arms, like children on Christmas morning.

"I missed you guys," he said, holding them both closely. They held onto him like a life preserver that's keeping them from drowning.

It took them a while before they noticed his companions.

Jameria asked, "What're you doing here?"

The happy reunion was cut short.

Demarcus got all serious. "They're here because you need they're help. "Ella D. and Bozy called me when they figured a few things out on their own. It seems Motif lead them here under false pretense."

"I knew it," Cole said to no one in particular.

"I'm sorry, but I knew that already. What I meant was, what are they *still* doing here? I thought-"

"Because of Tatum," Bozy interrupted.

"When I first laid eyes on him, something kept nagging me that I met him somewhere before. But that was impossible. Yet, something kept pulling me to him. Motif already told El how much he despised his own son. Then after your mother and father-in-law started snooping through our stuff and trying to make plans with us to get you off the island, we contacted Elder Demarcus."

"We kept in contact while I was on my way back here," Demarcus said, picking up where Bozy left off. "And we discovered something amazing. "When you were about two months old, your biological father went to your grandmother to see if what Ms. Ella D. told him about you was true. Word had spread about you and the snakes. But your grandmother refused him entrance. But when he realized the rumors was true, he went back to your grandmother's house one night."

"I'd call your grandmother several times, but she refused to talk about or even share custody," Bozy said continuing. "I'd at least wanted to teach you how to use your gift, but after what I've witnessed, you needed no help. You're a natural," he said smiling. "Anyway, that night I went to her house, there was another man there. We had to be about the same age at the time, so I figured he was in his early twenties. His hair was cut short, but he defiantly was from here.

"He was standing on the porch beside your grandmother. Then all of a sudden he jumped off her porch gallery, running and tackling me to the ground. I laid there shocked, wondering what I did to him. He sat up with a small blade in his hand...but a very sad look in his eyes. He looked at me and said, "'I'm sorry. But she's much more important than just your love. Think of this as our gift to them both.'"

Bozy lifted his arm, showing a darker line across his sepia skin.

"Then he sliced through my arm. I was so stunned from the pain, I was watching in a daze as he used the same knife to slice through his own arm. Moving quickly, he pulled a bottle from his pocket, poured some powder in his hand, then blew it in my face. I became dizzy, my vision blurry, but in all that, I thought I saw the man walk back to your grandmother, giving her the knife."

"I didn't realize he was talking about Tatum's father until he mentioned the mark behind his ear. Somehow Dominque knew Tatum belong to him and went to your grandmother for help," Demarcus said, grabbing Jameria's shoulders. "There's an old tale amongst our people about a cursed knife. A little different from what that old woman told you in the bookstore. This knife was used to kill several animals, different people. The blade is supposed to have been blooded many times over. In the tale was a woman who practiced black magic and used the knife to seek vengeance for those who was slain in vain....but like I said, it's an old wives tale."

"But if that knife exists, who would have it," I said, thinking out loud to myself.

"Well, of course it would go to a museum or-"

"Or the leader of the country," Cole finished.

"Is it possible Ky had the knife the whole time and gave it to Dominique," Rubae' asked. I'd forgotten she was in the room.

Jameria mumbled something none of us could hear.

"What," Bozy asked. Whatever she said had him in a slight panic.

"I have the knife," she said aloud.

She went to her bed, stooped down and reached underneath, pulling out a box wrapped in bronze silk with her initials sewn in the material. She removed the belly chain she normally wore around her waist before she got pregnant, from around her neck. She searched until she found a unique shaped diamond. She inserted it in the funny shaped lock and it popped open. She reached in it and pulled out a short single blade knife. The blade itself was rusted. But at a closer look, instead of rust, it was dried blood.

Bozy took in a sharp breath. "That's it," he whispered. He walked to her slowly, taking the knife in his hands.

His fingers stroked lightly across the exquisite hilt.

"The last Mistress, as well as my grandmother, left a few things behind I might need. Pat Ann taught me a lot of secret recipes. Some of those recipes is repeated in Ky Flask diary. There's no question that they knew each other. Dominique was keeping in contact with Ky. She told him she was pregnant with his baby. He tried to convince her to come to him. But she was loyal to her father and her people. So to keep her alive Dominque went to the States with the small fortune Ky gave him. During his stay in New Orleans, where he thought he was going to live out the rest of his life without the woman he loved, the rumors about me had spread. Dominique heard. And yes....he was very curious. Another person possessing a gift like *his*."

"Wait. Tatum's biological father is-"

"Yep.....just like me. Just a different animal."

"The wolves," Cole whispered. "Tatum."

"That's when he found Pat Ann. Ky didn't go into detail about Dominique's conversation with my grandmother, but I can just imagine," she said, easing the knife back out of Bozy hands. "Tatum's father couldn't get close enough to teach him. He was worried about his son with such an uncontrollable gift.....and an easy target for Motif. I guess all of you see where I came in at."

"Oh, God. What was Ky thinking? Tatum is already having sporadic episodes. You're a snake charmer. What Tatum can do, don't even have a name for it."

"It's mentioned in Ky's diary as a 'puppet master.'"

"Jameria," Demarcus began, reaching for the box. "What-"

She placed the knife in the box and slammed it shut. "Dad look, I wish I could tell you more, but I can't. She left me specific instructions to follow. And though you was a cool uncle and her best friend, she couldn't share it with you because it meant you being in danger, too. But I can tell you this, you helped her when she needed you the most," Jameria said, holding the belly chain up to Demarcus. "Do you remember the day you bought me this?"

He smiled reminiscing. "Yes. Tatum wanted you to have a welcoming gift. He pointed out the belly chain and asked me to buy it……Wait a minute. The jeweler."

"What about her," I asked intrigued. So many people went through so much to protect our Chief and Mistress. It almost seem surreal.

"The jeweler. The one who sold me the chain, use to be a servant here at the palace. Right after Tatum's birth, I never saw her again," Demarcus said, still looking down at the jewel. "I didn't recognize her at first, but I'm sure she knows who I am." Then Demarcus burst into laughter. "The jeweler was also one of Tatum and Karden's tutors. They was at the counter telling her about the special girl Tatum found to be his mate…..Now that

I've notice, I haven't seen her in there since the day we bought this chain."

"You said you hadn't seen her since the jewelry store and before that, the day Tatum was born. Was she the servant that delivered Tatum?" El was sitting close to Bozy on the edge of the bed.

Out of the corner of my eye, I saw the male snake charmer flinch whenever Jameria referred to Demarcus as 'dad.' Ella D. would squeeze his knee in comfort.

"No. She was the servant of Ky's left-hand man, who wasn't a man at all. Motif didn't think something like that was important, so he left that choice in Ky's hand. She chose a woman. Pierce's mother, I think."

Something made me look at Jameria as Demarcus spoke. I've seen her wear so many looks. Something the Elder said, confirming an unanswered question.

"How do you know about the 'Birthing Ritual,'" Demarcus asked. "It's a closed ceremony. Only the elders know about it. And they are going to be the only ones in attendance."

"Let's just say the former Chief was trying to make me an offer he didn't think I'd refuse. He was telling me his plan about how he was going to get rid of Merry during that birthing thing, before I had the chance to say 'hello' good."

"He told you? Then we can get him exiled off the island for good. It's treason to-"

"It's not going to work. The elders are already investigating our pack. Motif is claiming Tatum leads a violent pack……Dad, so much has occurred since you've been away."

"Well I'm here now," he said, squeezing Cole's shoulder.

"Merry. I know why you don't won't nothing to do with us, but we still want to help you. No matter where you go or what title you hold, you're still one of us. We Cajuns don't take fucking with kin too lightly." Ella D. got up from beside Bozy and kneeled in front of Jameria. She pulled a folded envelope from the inside of her shirt. "Here. This is your safe haven. It's a huge piece of land. A hundred acres to be exact, in a secluded spot in the bayou of Louisiana. You and your brothers and sisters can live there and raise your children in peace."

Oh God…Please God make her take it….This is the answer to our prayers….Please get us off this island.

Jameria placed her hand on Ella D's cheek. She place her hand on top, holding it there. "Thank you. And it's not that I didn't want anything to do with you. I was just trying to keep you safe. The less I knew about you and refuse to be near you, will keep Motif's suspicions at bay. It was just a show…that I don't think worked too well," she said looking at Bozy.

He smiled to himself, remembering their little confrontation.

"Be that as it may," Demarcus said, leaning against the bed post. I think you should take the gift your mother and father is offering. Get the pack together and get the fuck off of this island." He went to Jameria, placing his hand on her swollen

241

belly. "My grandson cannot lose his mother and Tatum cannot lose his wife." He kissed her cheek. "I cannot lose my daughter."

"Dad," Jameria said, shaking her head. "I have to go through the ritual. Think about it. Tatum's mother died to get us to this point. She manage to stay alive long enough to make sure her son was safe. And Pat Ann gave me to supposedly strangers, whom she tied my whole life to. I don't want all of their sacrifice to be in vain."

"Sweetheart, until you give birth, Motif and Boaz will be looking behind every bush and looking under every rock to find you. Please take the deed from your mother and leave this place. I'll admit, even I was surprised when they told me Ky survived. But Luv, you're taking a big chance if you think that will happen again."

Jameria searched the room until her eyes collided with mine. "I'm willing to take that chance."

I didn't like where this was leading.

I made my excuses and left.

Halfway down the hall, I heard the door open and close behind me. I turned and saw Jameria hurrying to me.

"They make a tempting offer," I said as she walked towards me.

"I never said I wasn't going to take it."

"Oh?"

She smiled. "I gotta plan and I'm going to need your help."

Chapter 18

Boaz.........

The pull was light, but I felt it just the same. Shy and I had just made it back home. As soon as our yacht docked, I felt it. I told Shy to cloak herself and go straight to my chambers. "And if need be, drop a boulder on anybody who gets in your fucking way."

I exited the boat, being guided by the pull. I didn't see him until I walked to the darkest shadow just inside the woods.

"Hello little brother. Did you enjoy your trip?"

Tatum.

He stepped out of the shadows. His long black hair cascaded around his shoulders like a black shawl. Sweat dripped from his six foot five inch frame, like he ran the longest marathon. But his breathing was even, like he didn't have a care in the world.

I stood my ground, trying not to show my nervousness. "Tatum. It was nice of you to be here to welcome me."

He tilted his head to the side. His perfect features glowing in the late Brazilian sun. "Ah, Boaz. How did we get to this point? Where exactly did we lose each other at?"

Really? Do he really want an answer or was that a rhetorical question?

"I think it was around the time you started fucking the woman I wanted. I know I wasn't of age yet, but I didn't have to be a rocket scientist to know you would let me keep both of my hands if I touched her. You've always been a selfish person. But you can't help it. It's just part of your nature. That's where the mistake came in on your part. As Jameria's left-hand man I was supposed to be just as close to her as you are. That's what pack members do. They share."

"Little brother," he said shaking his head. "Where did you get trash like that from? Motif?" He locked me in his gaze. His hazel eyes penetrating mine. There was something different about him. He seem more……..formidable. "So you turn your brother and sister out, made your mate a fashionable hoe, and plotted with Motif, all because you want my woman?"

I was angry now. He was making me sound like a kid having a temper tantrum. "She was not your woman until you laid with her. Do you know how it felt watching you and her having sex? Watching you shove your dick down her throat? I hated you for that! I hate you even more now since you destroyed her body with your spawn!"

Tatum shoved his hands in his pockets, took a couple of steps toward me and said, "Jameria became like a mother to all of us, but it had to be my own brother who misunderstood what motherly love was. Doesn't matter. You're no longer a part of my pack, so *you* don't matter. Anyway, I just wanted to get in a minute of private time with you, before the rest of the pack arrive."

"What?"

He looked at me like I asked the most ridiculous question. "Really, Bo?

Fuck what me and you are going through. Did you really think you was just going to slide by after what you put Pierce and Carmen through?"

At those words, one by one, they began to step out of the shadows. Colefirst, next Karden, Moham, and then Tyvine. They saved the best for last. Pierce stepped out last, accompanied by two wild wolves. Is it me or have all of them gotten bigger in just a few months.

Hmm, I haven't been able to attract the animals like I use to. At first I thought my little gift was natural. Now I know it was Jameria. She must have passed it on to Pierce. Along with the wolves were the two snakes Jameria received at the beginning of her pregnancy. They were wrapped snuggly around Pierce's arms.

"Hello brothers. Oh, that's right. You kicked me out, so we're no longer brothers," I said sarcastically.

"Bo," Karden said. "It seems to me you have no shame for what you put us through. Even your on brother, and he's your blood, Boaz. Did you want that title so bad to lose what you had with us?"

"How can I make you understand? It's about more than the title. Of course, I'll make a way better Chief than my older brother, here. But like Motif said, if I want something bad enough, I have to stand on my own two feet to get it."

"Well you can't stand alone forever, so that must mean your father is going to help you achieve those goals," Tyvine said, crossing his arms over his bared chest. I felt my own chest go hollow at the realization of what's about to happen.

"Oh, I see. It finally hit you, little brother," Tatum said smiling. "You're about to follow your father into the abyss."

"He's your father, too. You might not like it, but you share Motif's blood just as much as I do. Whatever his weaknesses are, you're sure to have them, too."

All of them stared at Tatum, waiting to see what he'll say next.

"Okay Bo," he said simply. "Guys, let's go. Our little brother would like some alone time with Boaz."

They all smiled. Pierce's the brightest. "Thank you," he said to Tatum as they all passed him heading back to the shadows of the forest.

I stared at him for a long moment.

"Boaz."

"Pierce," I said in greeting. "It's been a while. You've grown a lot since the last time I saw you."

"Well Bo, I am older than you….yet, you manage to make me and my mate into your sex slaves."

"Don't you think you're taking this victim shit a little too far? You got our brothers ready to rip my throat out."

His smile was mocking me. I watched as he opened the palm of his hands, signaling the snakes to slither in his long hair and the wolves to back off into the forest shadows.

How the fuck was they doing that? "It seems, I've missed out on a lot since I been away."

"More than you know, Bo. But seriously. Aren't we done with the small talk?"

"I guess you're right. Don't won't to prolong this ass whippin," I said arrogantly.

I didn't see him coming.

His combination of jabs, elbow and knee thrusts, had me dizzy. I didn't know where he was going to hit me next and with what he was going to hit me with.

He was dancing me to my death.

I tried to gather that inner strength that would take over my body whenever we trained, but I know now that was some kind of pull from either Jameria or Tatum when I was a part of the pack.

Within minutes, I was on the ground trying to cover my bruised face with my bruised hands.

A strong gust of wind blew us both against the hard old oak.

Standing, cloaked in black with a red bustier on, was Shy holding a fire ball.

"What a waste," she said looking at Pierce from head to toe. She walked up to him, placed her hand on his chest and let her fingers slide down his muscled abdomen, to his crotch.

"I'm going to miss this," she said, rubbing the huge bulge between his legs. She had Pierce pinned against the huge oak Jameria planted years ago in memory of her grandmother. Shy had him bound to the tree with strong vines.

Her gift is the four elements. She can control it, if her freaky side didn't get in the way. Her biggest weakness.

"Could you hurry the hell up? I gotta meet Motif," I said, running my swollen fingers across my face.

"Sorry Pierce, but Bo is more important than you will ever know. Don't worry. I'll make sure your girl joins you-"

Jade had Shy, spinning her in circles and wrapping around her body in a bear hug.

Jameria stepped out of the shadows. Motherhood had her glowing. Her swollen breast and round belly, made her look even more beautiful in her white silk cloak, as I imagined her pregnant with my baby.

"I could crush you, you know? I could crush your whorish bones right here, bitch. Have Jade to swallow your nasty ass whole and

I'll never have to see you again," she said. Her glare shooting daggers at Shy.

"Really? Really, Jameria? Do you really think your country ass can run an island? Hell, you're from the backwoods, bitch. But that's how you get your way with these people. Cajuns are known to have a strong magnetism of charm. You just exploit yours and let it go to your head."

Jameria held up her right hand and began closing her fingers into her palm, like she was squeezing something.

Shy cried out in pain. Her body too constricted to use her gifts.

The vines around Pierce loosened. He caught himself right before he hit the ground.

Jameria told a struggling Shy, "Behave bitch and I might give you an easy death." Pierce got up and went to our Mistress, circling his arms around her body, leaning in for a tight embrace. He stepped back, placing his hand on her middle, like the fucking unborn brat is his.

I was boiling hot at their show of affection. "I guess he's your left-hand man now that I'm out of the pack, huh Mistress?"

She looked at me and gave me that killer smile, still wrapped in Pierce's arms. "No."

Surprised and speechless.

To be the left-hand man of the Mistress means they share a special bond. One where when I came of age, I would've been trained to die for her. Her closeness to Pierce is way more intimate than I ever shared with her. As I stand here now, I'm wondering who could be closer than Pierce, other than Tatum.

Jameria stared at me as if she was reading my mind. "Pierce is Cougar's left-hand."

Oh God. "That means……"

Tyvine stepped out of shadows. A sardonic smile dominating his beautiful features, like the best gift you can give him is my death.

Jameria knew, other than Tatum, Tyvine is the second person I try not to fear. He and his mate believe in slow, agonizing torture. Torture so bad, I can still hear the man's horrendous cry, begging for someone to pleas kill him. And over the period of time I haven't been around them, make them all look even more formidable. But that's obvious observation. They've all grown in their skills too.

"Looks like I missed out on a lot of training with you guys. As you can see, my mate and I is no match. But I do promise you this Mistress, we will not come after you or the pack. You gave us the ultimatum to either train with the monks or challenge you as we are now. My mate and I decided to accept the challenge. One month after you give birth."

"One month?"

"Given how skilled you are in your gift, I think one month is justifiable. But if you die during the ritual, we will give my brother three months," I said smiling.

Jameria's smile brighten. "So we're making wagers now, Bo? You don't think I will make it. That's what you're betting on," she said bobbing her head in understanding. Her smile was so bright, it was like I offered her a deal of a life time. "How about we make it interesting. If I survive the 'Birthing Ritual,' I will not challenge you or your mate. You both can take on my mate at the same time, whenever you choose."

I thought a moment. It sounded too good to be true. Tatum won't survive if Shy and I was fighting together.

Something is up. "What's the catch?"

"Nothing. The only thing I want is for our agreement to be put in writing and that my sisters don't have to go through the ritual if I make it."

That bitch. "I see. You do know, even if you survive the ritual, if Tatum loses you and your entire pack will be exiled from this island."

"We know the consequences Bo, as long as you know them, too."

Tyvine walked up to Jade and let his fingers glide across her black scaled body. "Maybe next time girl. Let her go. We'll find something tasty for you. This one might give you gas."

Jade released her hold on Shy, letting her body fall to the ground in one heap.

Tyvine pulled my mate up by her hair and tossed her to me like a ragdoll. "Here's your bitch. Karden will be at your chambers later with the agreement in writing. After tonight, you won't lay eyes on our Mistress again until after she gives birth. Please don't hesitate to pass the info on to your father. We don't won't no misunderstandings if someone was to get hurt."

The three of them turned and went back into the shadows, following the huge snake.

I looked at my mate all balled up in the fetal position. "Dammit Bo, they're going to kill us!"

I knew that already, but I couldn't think about it right now. Tyvine became the Mistress left-hand. He's more close to her than anyone will ever be, other than her husband.

They did it to mock me. Or……. Could it be that Tatum and Jameria is nervous about someone getting to them, that they got 'The Torture Two,' guarding her?

Motif.

"Get up. We need to find my father."

"For what? He's depending on *you* to help *him*. We need to get our asses back on that boat and get the hell out of here. Did you feel the energy coming from them?"

"Think about it Shy. *Tyvine* is Jameria's let-hand. Not Pierce, not Moham, not even Cole. Do you know what that means?"

She thought a moment. "Either they're fucking with you or they're afraid of something...and it's something big." She eased up on her knees and stood. Pain etched across her face. "That country bumpkin bitch is going to pay for this shit."

~~~

Motif's chambers was empty. After locking Shy in my suite, I went to the last place I wanted to go.

Noonie's wing was lit up like a Christmas tree. Her rooms was located in the back of the palace now, close to the stables and pins. Tatum had all of her stuff moved off the main hall as soon as he became Chief.

The stench of animal-shit was riding the wind on this end of the palace.

Motif's guard and right-hand man was standing in the entrance, talking. They both glanced at me, but neither offered a word of welcome to see their former Chief and pack leader's son. I wonder if Motif had any followers left. I could hear him yelling and screaming at the top of his lungs. Once he laid eyes on me, his ranting and raving ceased.

"Boaz," he said as relief washed over his face. We held each other in an awkward embrace, releasing each other quickly.

Honestly, I have no love for Motif, but if he believes in me so much that he's willing to take out his first born, then I *must* be gifted. Even more powerful than Tatum.

"We have much work to do," he said without words of greeting.

I nodded my head.

"But first I need to know something."

Shit. He had that same look in his eyes Jameria and Tatum had since Shy and I departed the plane months ago.

The look a person give you when they've been betrayed.

"Did you know that Jameria was pregnant, before you left the island?"

Really? Did he really think I was so low as to conspire against a fucking fetus? I consider that type of shit as being sick. That was his problem, not mine.

Yet, I have enough enemies and Motif will not be one of them. "No. I didn't find out until months after the wedding." God, please don't let him know differently.

"We've been deceived, son," he said, placing his hand on my

shoulder. "Your brother didn't tell his own blood the Mistress is with child. All of these secrets he's keeping is proof he's not fit to run this island."

"Dad, did you know Tyvine is standing as Jameria's left-hand?"

Motif looked flabbergasted. "What?!"

I told him everything that went down from the time I stepped off the boat.

"And you're sure Tyvine is standing at her side?"

"My mate is in my chambers now, with a black and blue body. Jameria was Jade's alpha, Tyvine was the snake's omega," I said just as stunned as he was. "The snake obeyed him as if he was Jameria. More experienced than I ever was." I didn't mention that when I was a part of the pack standing by Jameria's side, Jade refused me as her omega then, too.

Maybe the reptile have some kind of six sense.

"They're nervous about something," he said more to himself than to me.

Noonie had left out of her own room, as soon as I entered.

The bitch found out I had her maids lacing her food with cleaning products. Now she know why she haven't been healing since her ass whipping she received from our beloved Mistress herself. But the bitch is right to run, because this shit ain't over until she takes her last breath.

"It doesn't matter," Motif continued. "King Kong can be her fucking foot, for all I care. I just want that bitch and her pack of freaks gone!"

I use to wonder why Shy was never included in Motif's version of 'freak.' But that only lasted a minute, knowing Shy probably sucked him off a couple of times. His days of marrying me off to the richest islands ended the day he met her.

"We have to get rid of that bitch before or during the ritual...."

"During, since you're the only one of us who can attend the ritual," I said. I went on to tell him about the agreement Jameria and I made.

He laughed like he was the happiest man in the world. "Killing two birds with one stone. Not only will Jameria die, all of her female pack will follow her to hell. Smart Boaz." He looked at me with admiration. "You're destine to be Chief of this island."

The next day, after a long night of strategizing and planning, I stood before Council in an urgent meeting. I can tell by the look of surprise on most of their faces that they didn't know of my return. Demarcus and Marlease (for some reason) looked down right pissed.

Motif had contacted Mara the night before, strongly advising him to call this meeting. After prayer, Mara went to the podium and asked all the right questions, which lead me to believe him and Motif must've rehearsed it several times.

"Is this true, young Boaz? Were you threaten," Mara asked, after Motif described my hellacious upbringing, led by a tyrant who was no more than a child himself.

"Of course it's true, Elder. You've seen for yourself the chaos the young couple is capable of." Noonie stood on the other side of me, presenting herself as my mother. *Boy,* I wish I could slap this bitch. I wanted to beat her ass just for breathing. "Jameria was dangerous from the moment she came to this island. And Tatum has been out of control since his early training years. Now they're about to raise a child like that. There is no doubt about it, Boaz will make a better leader when he comes of age."

"So you don't plan on honoring the agreement between you and the Mistress," Elder Gramz asked, cutting Mara off like he was nothing more than a servant.

"What?" How the fuck..... Karden never said he was going to Council with this so soon. Hell, I just signed the last document hours ago. When did he have time to do this? "I'm sorry, elder......I don't under-"

"Karden dropped these documents off to us with a recorded conversation between you and Jameria."

"I never received such document," said Mara.

Gramz stared at him. Analyzing his sudden mood change. "He told me to give you your copy," he said, handing Mara the brown package. "He'd already delivered to the other elders and by the time he came to my doorstep it was almost dawn. He asked me if I minded passing yours along.... Is something wrong Mara?" Gramz has always been fair. But Mara's attitude is going to have him asking a lot of questions, later. "Anyway, from the signed documents and the conversation on tape, the agreement between the two is sound."

"We thought you wanted to meet today young Boaz, to confirm your signature," Demarcus said, smiling. "Since there was a witness present, we saw no reason to wait for Mara, so we all signed, granting your request, with one exception. No blood or guardian is allowed in the ritual."

OH, that bitch!

"What?!" Motif's face was so red, I thought his heart was going to give out. "What witness?"

"Pierce."

This is so fucked up. Even if I don't confirm the signature, the papers are still legal because the fucking elders signed already.

Fuck it.

I went to the podium, grabbed the fucking pin and held it.Gramz: "You do know that if this agreement plays in your favor young Boaz, former Chief Motif will have to be acting Chief, until you come of age."

I threw a quick glance at Motif and saw the joy play havoc in his eyes.

Fuck it.

I X'd the document, verifying my signature and jumped off the podium.

Oh, that Jameria is an evil bitch. If I didn't love her so much I'd kill her ass, right now. How the fuck are we supposed to get in the ritual, now? She might not live....I'ma have to depend on that. But if she makes it.....I'll need a way to draw her out while she's still weak.

When I went and stood between the two idiots again, Motif patted me on the shoulder like I did something good. "Don't worry. I'll hire the best trainers in the world. Tatum won't be able to lay a hand on you. You're better than him. Remember that."

Is he really that clueless? Don't he realize Jameria is setting both of our asses up? I wanted to get the hell out of there.

I was about to make my excuses and leave, when Cole came through the door heading straight for the podium.

"What is it, young Cole," Gramz asked, stopping him in the middle of his stride.

Demarcus was already on his feet, moving around the other elders to get off the stage. Something in Cole's eyes had him elbowing a few of them in his rush.

"It's Jameria, elder. She's in labor."

Chapter 19

Tatum…………

I stood in the dressing room, fantasizing about me running away with my mate while my worst nightmare was becoming reality right in the next room.

I dressed down in white silk balloon trousers. Underwear is not necessary in the ritual. I walked into the open room. Tears coursed down my cheeks as I watched the pain etch across my mate's beautiful face. In the next room, Elder Demarcus, along with Ella D., and Bozy, lay sedated behind a locked door. It took all of my brothers to hole them down while Pierce injected them with something Jameria threw together just for this occasion. The rest of the elders stood around, encouraging Jameria to relax, take deep breaths……lying to her by telling her everything is going to be alright.

Over in the corner, I watch Pierce prepare the sacred tea. Jameria screamed, "Now," and something in my little pack brother changed. He threw me a quick glance before he went back to preparing the tea. He had several cups on a tray, surrounding a tea pot and a bottle of *'Camus Cognac Cuvee,'* he presented to the elders one at a time. When he made it to me and presented the little tea cup, only then did I remember those four words he spoke to me months ago.

"'Don't drink the tea.'"

I spoke loud enough for the Elders to hear. "I'm too nervous Pierce, I don't think I'll be able to hold anything down."

"Here," he said, balancing the tray with one hand. He passed me a cup at the very end of the tray that was slightly different from the rest of the cups. "This should keep you on your toes Chief."

I didn't second guess it. I took the cup and tossed the contents down, forgetting about the toast that was supposed to be made.

Pierce snatched the empty cup placing it back on the tray. He continued on before my eyes could clash with his. The contents in *my* cup was nothing more than watered down unsweet tea.

I looked around me wondering if anyone else noticed my special cup. All I saw was sympathy. That's understandable, since this might be the last time I see my wife alive.

"In honor of the new heir," Gramz announced. All of them held their cups in the air before they brought them back down to their lips, letting the warm liquid coat their bellies.

Jameria screamed again, this time a lot more agonizing. The elders hurriedly took their seats to watch the perverted ritual.

I removed my pants and stood naked before them. They stared at my huge dong as if it held them in a daze. Then I noticed a real change in their eyes. Like they was here....but wasn't. They all set as still as statues. Just staring at the entertainment before them, with no emotion.

"Chief," Pierce said. He grabbed my arm, guiding me to the birthing table so I could take my place under Jameria.

"What did you do to them," I whispered.

"Not now," he lifted Jameria's shoulders a little so I could slide in behind her easily, with one leg on each side of her. Right before he covered us with a sheet, he whispered, "No penetration."

I threw a quick glance at the audience and saw the astute elders had yet to bat a lash.

II fumbled around with my dick, lifting Jameria as if I was entering her from behind. Another contraction hit in time to make the roost look real. As I held onto my wife while the contractions took over her body, Pierce was moving around under the sheet at the other end of the table. I felt him mash something into our joined hands, under the sheet and from our waist down, the sheet turned blood red as another contraction shook my mate to the core.

Realizing what Pierce was doing, I released one of my hands from Jameria's ultra tight grip and spread the red goo between both of our thighs. As if on cue an unemotional Nuieve came to the birthing table to do his inspection. Pierce raised the sheet just enough for him to peep under. I don't know what he saw, but he gave a slight nod to the rest of the elders, indicating I had indeed penetrated my wife. After he returned to his seat, Pierce went back to work under the sheet just as the Mistress next contraction hit.

"It's time to push now, Jameria," Pierce said, looking at us over the huge bulge.

Jameria strained and pushed for what felt like hours, sometimes screaming myself, just imagining her pain.

"I see the head, he announced. "Okay Mistress, one big push and you're home free."

With all the strength she could muster, plus with my help, Jameria gave a strong push, screaming from the top of her lungs. Her nails dug into my hands as she strained to bring the new life into the world. Soon the room filled with another loud wale.

"It's a boy!"

Jameria's body fell limp against my chest as she took in deep breaths. Before Pierce could lay my son upon her chest, something had him down between her legs again, working at a frantic pace. Jameria gripped my hand again, holding tight, but saying nothing. Just gritted her teeth.

The door to the waiting room opened and Moham appeared coming to Pierce's aid.

What the fuck is going on?

Soon Jameria's grip loosened and Moham carried a wrapped bundle back to the waiting room with him. Only then did Pierce bring my son and lay him upon my living wife's chest. Whatever her and Pierce did, they've manage to pull it off. I just hope our zombie elders reclaim their senses in time for the celebration.

I looked over my mate's shoulder and stared down into surprised eyes like mine. His skin was a light golden brown with a head full of black curls. His full pink lips made an O as if he was just as surprised to see me.

Too beautiful……too beautiful to stay on this fucked up island near Motif. As soon as my living mate is strong enough, were getting the fuck off of this cursed land.

Motif can have this bitch!

~~~

Wrapped in fresh linen robes, I followed Tyvine, carrying my infant son as he carried my living wife. For the second time in history, another Mistress survived the 'Birthing Ritual.'

The people of Geri Island filled the courtyard to throw flowers and jewels at our feet. Many were snapping pictures and passing camcorders back and forth to show they was present, during this monumental event. The precession to the palace was long, yet comfortable, but when we made it to the north wing, I think I heard Tyvine sigh in relief.

Pierce hurriedly closed and locked the gate behind us, before hurrying ahead to open and close the double oak doors, also. The mates were in the hall, smiling with their hands on their own bulging bellies. Tyvine entered our suite, heading straight for the bedroom. He placed Jameria on the bed and folded the covers over her. Her eyes opened slightly, scanning the room for someone in particular.

The entire pack had filed in behind us. So when they finally touched Moham she said, "Bring him to me." I gave Pierce my son to hold, until I climbed in the bed next to Jameria, confused as to what she meant.

Moham came back in the room with a bundle he held as precious as a jewel. A slight cry came from my son, until the bundle in Moham's arms whimpered in protest.

My breath caught.

Moham laid the bundle in Jameria's arms. She smiled ever so gently. I looked down into her cradled arms and saw the identical face of the baby mirrored in my arms.

I stared into Jameria's sleepy eyes. She smiled and said, "Name?"

I smiled back. It was no question about the infant in her arms. He entered the world so gracefully, so quietly, it was like living art. "Poet."

The infant in my arms let out a loud wail to say he needed thesame attention. His wail sounded more like a song. "Lyric."

I sat up in bed, laid Lyric before me and retrieved Poet out of his sleeping mother arms. I laid the twins side by side, staring down at the identical faces before me.

To no one in particular I said, "Explain."

Pierce took a deep breath and said, "She knew she was pregnant with twins the day Demarcus made it back to the island. Ella D told her in private to expect it. Since I was the one delivering the babies, she had to tell me."

"She told me the same day," Moham continued. "She came out into the hall and asked me to do something very important for her. She told me after the birth of the first baby, she needed me to retrieve the second. That's when I knew."

Pierce came and knelt beside me and said for my ears only, "That was the only way we could make the ritual look real and protect her at the same time."

I grabbed him in a bear hug. This young man helped me keep my entire family alive. There is nothing in this world I can give him to ever repay a debt like that. "Thank you."

The mates climbed on the bed and started passing the twins around with oohs and ahhs. I followed my brothers out into the sitting room, closing the bedroom door behind me. Tyvine went to the fridge and pulled out a bottle of champagne while Karden, Moham and Pierce rolled fat blunts to celebrate the happy occasion.

"The elders are throwing you a bigger shindig later on the beach. This right here brother, is for immediate family only," Karden said smiling from ear to ear. He was more than overjoyed.

Our Mistress has manage to live through the 'Birthing Ritual,' and in the process, she saved her sisters from seeing the same faith.

Tyvine went to Pierce, passing him the first glass of champagne. "Sorry Chief, but the first glass have to go to our little brother who worked miracles today."

If he only knew.

I grabbed a glass of the bubbly, snatched the fatty out of Pierce's hand and lit it, taking a long pull. "Sorry man, but in another year, you'll be making your own baby. So none of this for you."

"Ah man. That's fucked up," he said flopping down on the couch.

We all laughed, enjoying the happy mood until the loud pounding decided to interfere.

I removed the bedroom key from around my neck, locking the occupants inside. Karden went to the sitting room door to let the intruders enter. If it was Motif, he can come in, but he won't be leaving back out.

Once we saw that it was Demarcus with Ella D. and Bozy, we relaxed a little.

Only a little.

Something about the look in Ella D's eyes had me removing the key again and giving it to her. She took the key then walked around me to enter the bedroom.

Demarcus took the blunt out of my hand taking a long drag of his own, before passing it on to Bozy. "I needed that," he said, releasing the pinned up smoke. "You damn kids is going to turn me gray before I'm old." He flopped down on the couch beside

Pierce, taking the boy's drink and swallowed the contents in the glass in one gulp. "You haven't even made a kid yet and got the nerve to be drinking. Get up and get me something stronger."

"Dad, are you alright," Cole said, grinning. "I can't tell if you're happy or pissed."

Demarcus took the glass of cognac from Pierce before he looked at his son and said, "Fuck you."

"He sounds more livid than pissed," Tyvine said, edging them on.

"You dicks sedate me, yet you expect me to come to you with smiles and hugs. You lucky I'm not kicking nobody's ass right now," he said taking another gulp of his drink.

My eyes strayed to Bozy, who sat quietly, hitting the weed.

Jameria told me about the conversation she had with her biological father and her stepfather. After I heard the full story in detail, I understood Bozy a little more. The man was willing to die for a daughter he had never been able to hold. And now, years later he's still fighting for his child, even though another man raised her and is still a very important part of her life. The man must be in pure agony.

I went to Bozy and asked him to join me in the bedroom. My brothers stared at me confused, but uncle Demarcus nodded his head in agreement. He understood even if my brothers didn't.

Jameria was sitting up in bed learning how to breast feed to Ella D's coaching. The mates was sitting in a circle learning as much as they could from watching. "Excuse me ladies. Can we have a moment with Jameria and the twins?"

They all filed out, Ella D. handing me little Poet in passing. I closed the door quietly and went to my wife watching her pop her nipple out of greedy little Lyric's mouth. His pink lips was still shaped like the letter O as if he was still suckling on the nipple. I placed Poet in her free arm to be fed, while I burped Lyric. I watched Poets eyes close as if he was in ecstasy once his lips fasten around the milk chocolate areola.

I know how he feels.

Jameria used a white baby blanket to cover his head and her breast as he fed. I looked back at Bozy who came a little closer to the bed. I decided to give them some private time.

I went into the closets, laid on the dressing room couch and fell asleep with my son napping on my chest.

I don't know how long I was out, but screaming from everywhere woke me out of a deep sleep. I looked down and saw my son still resting on my chest, but he wasn't alone. The baby gaboon who refused to leave Jameria's side during her pregnancy, was now wrapped around his little arm. And sitting on my chest next to him was the pup Chewy, I received as gifts from the alpha wolf.

The screams had me scooping everyone up and running into the next room. Ella D. was holding Poet protectively in her arms in the bathroom doorway, while Bozy and Demarcus did their best to hold a frantic Jameria down.

Pierce came to me and took my son out of my arms and went into the bathroom with Ella D., closing the door behind him.

"What the fuck is going on now," I yelled. But no answer was needed.

I felt it. As soon as I got close enough to my mate, I felt that painful jab in the middle of my chest.

Coral.

I ran out of the room passing my brothers and sisters at top speed, only to stop dead in my tracks at the unbelievable scene before me.

At the back of the palace at the edge of Noonie's wing, what remained of Motif's retired pack, had the large snake strung in the air skinning him alive.

The pain was so unbearable, I dropped to my knees. Tears clouded my vision as I watched Remy run the blade down the reptile's body removing his skin from his flesh.

The earth rumbling beneath my knees couldn't even move me. If Motif wanted me dead, now was his chance. But I never felt the blow come. Instead Tyvine ran pass me, followed by Karden, Cole, and Moham.

I turned when I felt a hand on my shoulder.

"Come on, Chief. You're stronger than this. Let your pain be your strength. Let the pain you feel right now take control of your entire being," Bozy whispered in my ear.

I let his words guide me, while the rest of my mind was focused on my pack. Then I looked at Coral once again. Saw his beautiful skin laying beneath him and the rage inside me took over my entire being.

The wolf call boomed from my voice like a nuclear bomb being dropped. Next to me, I heard the masculine sound of a loud hiss. Soon, Bozy and I was surrounded by wolves and snakes of all shapes and sizes.

Jade slithered forward, coiling her body around Bozy, lifting him off the ground. Seven anacondas lined side by side, waited for his command. On each side of me the alpha wolf and his mate waited on my signal. It wasn't until I saw my brothers being over taken, not only by Motif's pack, but several of his trusted guards, that I felt my rage was beyond control. I released a growl that had Tyvine flipping over Remy's head and snapping his neck in one motion. Behind me, I heard a man scream.

Motif was moving in close.

I could hear his machete whipping through the wind. Meanwhile, Bozy and I had Noonie's entire wing surrounded. Shitoba, one of the last three remaining members of Motif's pack, picked up the blade Remy was using before his instant death, to finish what the man started. The smallest snake among the anacondas, the one Jameria calls 'Chicken,' swooped down, twirled the man in his body and swallowed him whole, slowly without crushing his bones.

A slow torturous death.

I looked up Jade's long body and saw that Jameria mirrored Bozy in some ways, when it comes to snake dancing.

Motif went for the Chicken.

Running off anger and adrenaline only, I had the wolves cover Motif's body in a matter of minutes. I could hear them tearing and ripping through his flesh. Mangling him to an unrecognizable beast.

"That's enough Tatum! Stop! No matter what he's done, he's still our father!"

And only then could I calm my rage.

Boaz.

If Motif had told him the truth about our parentage, this scene would've played out until the end of him.

I would've ripped his throat out with my bare hands.

He went to Motif, checking for a pulse, while my brothers came to me blooded and bruised. Tyvine stared at me with a pained look in his eyes.

I knew what he had to do.

He's the omega to Jameria's alpha. I assigned him this dreadful task. He had to put Coral out of his misery.

At the mere thought of it, my sorrow took over and the wolves dissipated, returning to the woods as if nothing happened.

Bozy came to me and put his hand on my shoulder, looked at Karden and said, "Get him out of here. He don't need to see this. He'll feel the pain just the same."

 Karden and Moham had to literally drag me away. I looked back in time to see Boaz staring at Coral, as if he was in a state of shock. Then his eyes darted to me. That look will be the last, I'll remember him by.

"I'm sorry," he mouth, with tears streaking his cheeks.

 By the time we made it to the corner of the palace, I felt the last blow that ended Coral's life.

Chapter 20

Ella D……….

    I stood close to the kid beside me. He seem more like a grown man than a boy of seventeen. His muscular body was relaxed as he held my grandchild in his arms. Snakes slithered all over us in a caressing dance.

The boy Pierce has no fear.

I on the other hand was scared shitless. It took all of my mental ability to not shake with the baby in my arms. I stared at the boy again, trying to focus on anything but this de-ja-vu I'm reliving for the second time in my life.

The young man's breath caught. The snakes stilled. I wanted to look in his handsome face and see if he was alright, but his long jet black hair concealed him from my vision when he dropped his head.

Then the snakes were moving franticly, completely covering our bodies.

I couldn't take it anymore.

I went for the door handle, but the boy pulled me back as if the doorknob would've burned me to the touch.

"Not yet," he whispered.

    I stood there for what felt like forever. The child in my arms was asleep, breathing evenly, until a sharp cry from the other room had him joining in with his brother and the screaming in the next room. Someone snatched the door open from the other side. Tatum seized his baby out of my arms. The pained expression on his face almost broke my heart.

The boy Pierce walked out behind him. I followed, scanning the room. Jameria was lying on her side in the fetal position. Her pack sisters surrounded her, cajoling her. They glanced at me for a bet of a second before they made room on the bed, so I could comfort my daughter. I don't know what could have happen to make her and Tatum so upset, but I sat running my fingers through her hair. Then I glanced at Tatum, wondering what the hell he was doing. He'd grabbed several blankets from a pantry closet. After he spread the blankets on the floor, he placed the babies side by side, throwing another blanket over them. He got his knees before them and cover their eyes with his hands, before he looked back at Jameria and nodded.

Jameria sat up. She looked so tired. So worn. She raised her hands above her head, releasing a loud hiss into the air. The snakes scattered, lapping over each other to get as far away from this place as fast as they could. And just when I thought I'd seen and done enough in one day to last me a life time, a fucking snake the length of the Empire State building was slithering around outside the fucking window.

Bozy came through the door drenched in sweat.

He went to his daughter, pulling her in his arms. "I'm so sorry Jameria. Tyvine made it quick. He will not suffer anymore."

I wish someone will tell me what the hell is going on.

"The snake Jameria grew up with in the bayou is gone," he said as if he read my mind.

Demarcus came into the bedroom. He left right after the boys charged after their Chief. He glanced around the room. Saw Tatum, looked at Jameria, then his eyes landed on me. He took long determined strides toward me.

"Get them out of here. They have to leave now," he said in a frantic low whisper.

"But Jameria's not strong enough to leave, yet. She just gave birth hours ago. How can you make her leave when she's so weak?" I was as lost as a puppy.

"They are going to call a meeting. And when they call this meeting, they is going to prosecute Tatum as Motif's son. A blood heir who almost killed the former Chief of this land without witness. Right now, Motif is being shipped to the mainland. His injuries was too severe. If he don't make it, this won't be good for Tatum or Jameria. It will mean death for the entire pack."

"Oh God."

"And after seeing what Tatum can do, it only gives them more reason to make Boaz Chief. At least with Tatum missing, the trial can be postpone until he's found or Boaz comes of age. Tatum needs to find his real father before that happens. He needs to claim his birthright. And there's no way he can do that here."

This was the type of shit I've always tried to avoid in my life.

"Okay," I said, dropping my head in defeat.

"Do you have somewhere you can hide all of them? Somewhere, not even I know about?"

I thought a moment and came up with the perfect place. "Yes," I said enthused.

"Good. You should go pack. Meet me at the docks in one hour."

I grabbed Bozy, pulling him with me and talking as fast as I could, before he had me repeat myself several times. We had to get them kids off this Godforsaken island, without getting killed.

Damn. I should've stayed my ass in Vegas strippin.

~~~

An hour and ten minutes later, I stood on Demarcus private yacht, watching the cloaked figures approach the boat. One after the other, all twelve members with two infants boarded the boat, to let me take them off to only God knows where.

Demarcus boarded the boat, grabbing Merry and Cole in a bear hug. "This is not the end. I will find you when the time is right. In the meantime, help Tatum find Dominique. He's needed now, more than ever." He went to Tatum, held him in his arms as he whispered something in his ear, before he turned and left the boat. The rest of the pack went below after wishing him well.

Merry stood by the rails as the yacht departed the docks. I stood next to her, looking at the beautiful island as we gained distance from it.

"What's on your mind," I couldn't help but ask.

She smiled. She have such a beautiful smile. "I was thinking, why I have to be the one to finish what Vilmander started. Why did I have to be picked as Mistress to have such a burden like this?"

It was almost funny.

"Really Jameria? Do you know of a woman stronger than you?"

"Yeah…..but she died when I came to this ratchet ass place."

"Pat Ann knew you could handle it or she would've never sent you here."

"Well don't look like I'm doing a good job of it. I just had to pack my entire family up, because we was the main participants in a mass murder."

"Oh Merry, that ole Motif just knew how to get to you. There's no reason you should feel guilty for anything."

There was that smile again. She's even more breathtaking with that smile. "I haven't been called that since I was five-years-old. Grandma started calling me Jameria or Honey Chile." She let out an exasperated breath. "I really do miss her."

"Speak for yourself. After the day I had today, my first stop back home might be to a Mama's house to contact Pat Ann on the other side," I said. She burst out laughing imagining the scenario.

"Jameria, I'm sorry I wasn't there for you. I'm not going to make any excuses. I was young, what can I say?"

"You can say nothing at all. My life was planned before I entered this world and you had no knowledge of it. You was where you needed to be. You needed to be here today and here you stand. Now, enough of the mushy stuff, where are we headed," she said, leaning against the rails.

"Well there's that little hide-a-way. I think it will be right up your ally. But I have to tell you it will need a lot, and I do mean a lot of work."

Those honey brown eyes of hers, stared at me with skepticism.

"Don't worry Merry. You can handle it."

"Yeah. That's what they all say."

~~~

It took us a while to get settled in at Jameria's farmhouse. Bozy wanted their stay on the property to be as short as possible. We had to practically wrestle their cell phones away from them, fearing they might be traced back.

The Pack was ruthless.

Especially the pregnant ones. That damn Cougar almost bit my hand off when I tried to take the jar of honey from out of her grip. That damn girl ate so much honey, I had to keep sending the boys out to the combs to get more. I wouldn't be surprised if that child came out to be pure honey. What I couldn't believe was Demarcus put up with all these kids for years and still manage to look like a man in his early thirties.

My fear of my grandsons and their mother getting sick from the long traveling, was put aside. Instead they all flourished. The twins looked like angels. Huge hazel eyes set in smooth golden hue skin. Thick black curly hair. So beautiful. Jameria grew stronger every day. She's like Wonder Woman on steroids. She breast fed her babies, cooked meals for her family, trained with her brothers, trained with the snakes, train with her husband…..and the girl still had enough energy to please that beautiful ass man every night. I should know. My room was right next to theirs in the farmhouse. The walls are too damn thin.

A few weeks after everyone got settled in, Jameria, Tatum, Bozy, Karden, Tyvine, and me, went on the hike to the hide-a-way.

"So, the only way to this place is by boat," Karden asked navigating the single engine.

"Yeah….take a left here around the bank," I said, knowing he'll have to cut the engine soon. The vegetation was so thick and close, you can reach out and touch the greenery with your hands. "Cut the engine."

We drifted to what looked like a dead end.

"Are we lost?"

"No," Bozy said, looking at me. He nodded his head as if to say I did a good thing. "The canal is one big water maze. No one will be able to find you here. Let the boat drift through the trees. Don't forget to duck."

 The boys grabbed a few branches to pull us on through and the shock from the boat was like a scene from a movie, taking their breath away.

        The mansion was huge sitting on one hundred acres. The waterfall in the back of the house, which we now face, made the mood picturesque. Karden and Tyvine took the ores and rowed us the rest of the way. They walked up the rickety dock, taking their time exploring the place.

"You said the only way here is by boat," Merry said, examining the broken shutters and shattered glass. "How did they transport the material to build the mansion?"

"Underground tunnels. This use to be my great-great-great-grandfather's plantation." Bozy didn't say no more than that. He had planned to give her the plantation anyway as a wedding gift.

That's a secret I'll keep between us.

Tatum and his brothers came from exploring upstairs. Damn that boy looks like a young God. "It needs a lot of work, but I think we can manage."

"Are you sure," Bozy began. "You know there's no plumbing

and-"

"We got it covered," Tyvine said smiling. "We've done this before."

They all smiled knowingly at each other, leaving me and Bozy in the dark.

Epilogue

Tatum..........

Three years later.

"Harder…..harder……..

Jameria was riding me as hard as she rode Windspeed her horse. The Louisiana heat was bearing down on us. Her body sleek with sweat was tempting me beyond sanity. I rolled deep inside of her, pulling her down by her shoulders, forcing her to take it all in.

"Do you feel how much I love you," I said grinding even deeper. I rotated my finger in and out of her ass, suckling on nipples and drinking down her motherly essence.

I begged her to continue with the breast pump after the boys was old enough to stop feeding. Jameria consume so many strawberries, that I have strawberry milk *every* morning with my cereal. She removed herself from my long pipe, laid on her back and crossed her legs behind her neck.

So flexible.

Her pussy was so wet, the slurping sound was keeping tempo with the beat of the slow jam. She grabbed me around my neck, catching the rhythm and jacking my dick off with that fat ass pussy of hers.

The buildup was too excruciating to hold. "I can't it no longer, Merry," I said between clenched teeth. We'd picked up on her southern nickname quickly, after watching how her face changes whenever Ella D. let it slip.

Her muscles contracted, squeezing me so tight that each gush from my sensitive head, felt like a geyser exploding.

I collapsed on top of her, releasing her legs from behind her neck and replacing them with my arms. She proceeded to wrap her legs around my waist, snuggling me deeper inside of her. The alarm went off, indicating we only had a few minutes, before we were invaded. I leaned up on my elbows, starring at her beautiful face. Her thick black hair was spread over the pillow like a raven's wing. I kissed her soft lips slowly, but possessively. I felt myself getting hard all over again.

Bam! Bam! Bam! "Mama? Mama you in there? Daddy, is my mama in there?"

Dammit!

"Let me get up or he'll have everyone in the house up again," she said pushing me out of her.

She threw on a robe and I had the pleasure of watching her sashay to the bathroom while I slipped my pajama bottoms on over my hard-on. But it was quickly depleting since Lyric refused to stop beating on the damn door.

I snatched the door open in the middle of his banging. "What the fuck do you want?!" The little shit glared at me with my eyes. The gaboon viper he named Vinny, wrapped around his arm and

Chewy his wolf friend always by his side, don't look as if they awoke on their own.

At three years old, Lyric felt like he can control the world. The boy gets up at the crack of dawn and have the whole damn house buzzing. "Where's my mommy," he said walking pass me like he own the place.

"She's in the shower. Where's your brother? Go bother him for a while. Ask him to teach you some manners. That should keep you busy for hours."

"He's in his room, drawing. Can I train with you today? I promise I won't kick your ass, again," he said smiling.

Lyric and I had a bond from the moment he was born. That bond intensifies every time he watches me train with the pack. Recently, we started training before the sun makes an appearance to let the kids train with us, so the girls can have a little peace and quiet.

"Give me a minute to change," I said already heading for the closets. "And keep Vinny on your arm....I mean it Lyric. I don't want him running loose in this room.

I threw on a pair of jeans, not bothering with underwear and went back in the bedroom to find Tyvine and his daughter Beauty, sitting at the small kitchenette, eating my fucking cereal and milk. Little Beauty didn't have her panther cub, Cashmere at her feet, today.

"You can't say good morning before you start eating up my shit."

"Good morning," he said between bites. "Give me some juice."

I grabbed Lyric and Beauty and put them and the animal kingdom outside in Jameria's private garden, leaving the glass doors open. The morning breeze quickly filled the room. I grabbed the orange juice on my way back to the dinette.

"You know that's breast milk you're drinking," I said, sitting across from him.

He hunched his shoulders and continued eating, until he swallowed the last of his milk from the bowl. "Cougar kicked us out this morning.

Cashmere got into her thongs again." Cougar had threaten to kill the cub several times. But one look at her curly red head daughter with Tyvine's face, had Cougar melting on the spot.

"I was gonna take the boys out to train this morning."

"Good. We need to get out of the house, anyway. I saw at least six pounds of butterbeans that needs hulling. I don't want to be nowhere around when they start asking for help."

Come to find out what Boaz said about sharing my wife with her left-hand man, was true. The bond between the two had to be witnessed. Jameria and Tyvine made a video, showing we were still upholding the tradition to send to Council. To be fair and to pour salt on Boaz wounds, Tyvine let me fuck Cougar a few times. Sometimes participating in threesomes.....all with photo shop. We sent him a personal tape of his own. He can jack off to that shit, because as long as I'm living, he'll never touch Jameria.

I left Tyvine with the kids while I rounded up the rest of the fathers and children.

Once everything was decided, Bozy and Ella D. took up residence at Jameria's farmhouse to alert us of any danger. After two years of hard, backbreaking labor, we'd finally got the mansion restored. The equipment and the manpower was kind of tricky, but with the right amount of money, you can get just about anything done on the hush, hush.

We also had the tunnels restored.

After three massive floodings, we had two of the tunnels blocked off, using just the one in case of emergencies. We have several gardens, cattle, chickens, pigs, and horses, we raise and live off of, plus many accounts we have under anonymous names. It was needed since the house actually had no electricity before we restored it. The mansion had six columns on the top and bottom levels. Strawberry vines coiled around the columns creating a fairytale feel. The front of the house was one big green lawn with thick vegetation surrounding the opened space. Weeping willow trees scattered throughout the open space, gave the entire mansion a feel of comfort.

The house provided twenty bedrooms, each with their own private baths. Jameria and I had the servants quarters converted into our own master bedroom, which was also our panic room. Titanium was built into this side of the house. Our bedroom held a pool size bathtub and a king size bed inside the bath. All white and gold furnishing and plumbing and patio doors that stretch as one wall. But when the panic button is hit, metal shutters cover the complete glass. The bedroom itself was complete with a large kitchenette. Three custom made sofas that lets out into beds, faced the huge fireplace with the flat screen over the mantel. A gym room on the other the side of our closets and a playroom with several cribs and a large queen size bed in a nice size room next to the kitchen.

Inside the master suite itself, a custom made king size bed that you had to walk up four stairs to get to, was the main attraction. The bed was made to sleep at least thirty people. The anacondas ornately carved around the four posts almost touched the ceiling. The bed was made out of thick mahogany oak with white mosquito draping the entire bed. The headboard itself, had wolves hand carved into the wood. Three wolves on each side of the alpha wolf which held a large oval shaped mirror in its mouth.

Seven wolves. Demarcus told me a long time ago all packs have to have seven brothers. If I plan on going back to face Motif and Boaz, I'll have to find a seventh. *If* I decide to go back.

I walked down the long corridor, letting my bare feet sink into the thick carpet, stopping at Cole's wing of rooms first, before I headed up stairs. Jameria and I wasn't the only ones to have twins. Maria gave birth to Peace and Piper a few months after Beauty came along, who was born in the middle of a fucking hurricane, days after we made it to the States.

"What's up, man," I said, lifting Piper up in my arms. She has the same small features like mother, unlike her brother who reminded me so much of uncle Demarcus, I get homesick.

"Playing 2K. What's up with you," he said, still focused on the game.

"About to go train. Where's Peace?"

"Mo took him and Charm to see Xavier." Charm is Moham's two and a half year old son. Charm was born on the hottest night in June. Pierce was sweating bullets trying to bring him in the world. But once he came, his shocking green eyes with his toothless grin earned him his name.

Xavier is Pierce and Carmen's two year old, who was named after the very first school his mother and father attended. "What's wrong with Xavier?"

"Your son," Cole said, putting the controller on the mantel. He didn't have to say anything else. Lyric is known for getting into

mischief and little Xavier follows his lead.

"Pierce got him on punishment again?"

Cole laughed. "He's going to hate it, too. Xay loves training."

I put Piper on the floor, knowing her little legs is taking her straight to the kitchen where she sits and watch the women cook. "Ya'll coming," I said, heading for the door.

"Yeah," Cole said going into his bedroom. Let me get dress and I'll stop by Pierce and Karden's on my way."

Since he saved me from having to go upstairs, I went back through the kitchen and saw that Jameria, Maria, Tyce, and Kalanie preparing breakfast. The women held to their cackling as I went back to our quarters, to Poet's room.

Po is the opposite of Lyric. Always quiet and very caring and sincere when it comes to other people feelings. Unlike Lyric's room that's a constant mess, Poet kept his room more like an artist loft. The boy had crayon in his hands before he could walk. His thick wavy hair covered his head and shoulders like a shawl. The black mamba Venus, that was usually nestled in his hair, was stretched out on his window seat sunbathing. Lewie, his wolf friend, was used as a pillow while the furry animal slept in peace.

"Can I join you," I said sitting down beside him.

He put his crayon and his book down, stood and hugged me around my neck. "Hey Dad."

I circled my arms around his little body, holding him tight. "Hey, Po."

Just like Moham's son, Poet have the women in this house wrapped around his finger. At first, I thought the boy was going to be a loner, until I caught him staring at Karden twin daughters, Phoenix and Phoebe. Especially Phoebe. I caught on to my son's little fascination with the girl during training, when the two had a stand-off. Phoebe had a massive swarm of black birds about to attack him and he had pythons slithering out of the free running river, coming at her. The look in his eyes when he stares at her, reminds me so much of how Jameria looks at me during training.

He went to his dresser, got a brush and a rubber band, sat down between my legs and waited patiently until I brushed all of his hair in a ponytail. "Do you want to train with us today," I said, handing him the brush back. He was already running to his closet to change. I waited until he was done and said, "No training with the animals today. You and Phoebe almost scared your mothers to death."

He dropped his head, making me regret even that little chastisement. "Sorry dad."

I picked him up, went through my bedroom patio, out to the private garden where little Beauty and Lyric was sparing off, trying to follow Tyvine's coaching. Moham, Cole, Pierce, and Karden came up behind me, watching the two in a dance of battle.

Cole looked out towards the raging river. "What's that," he said, walking to the locked gate. It was Bozy and two unknown occupants traveling with him.

I put Poet down to join the rest of the children before I unlocked the gate and went down to meet Bozy at the dock. The closer I got to him, the more stressed he looked. We went to him quickly, grabbing the edge of the boat, pulling him to dock. I stared at the two occupants. They were defiantly from my island.

"I'm sorry, Tatum. Demarcus told me not to chance your safety, bringing you a message. So he told me to bring the package directly to you when it gets here. I had no idea he was talking about actual people."

I held out my hand to help the young woman off the boat and a beautiful little native girl peeped from under her mother's cloak, before she ducked back in, hiding again.

The young man said, "Her name is Barra. I'm Liam and this is my wife Claire. Your uncle Demarcus sent us. He told me to give this to the Chief and he would understand." He held up a blue silk scarf with a silver wolf sewn into the hem. I looked at Liam's massive chest that was restrained by a gray t-shirt, his straight black hair was in a ponytail and powerful legs sheltered in jeans.

Liam and his wife were in their early twenties like the rest of us. There was a scar that was just visible under the hem of his short sleeve. I could just imagine what he went through to cross Boaz just to stand by my side.

"Brothers," I called. "Let's welcome Liam to the pack."

Eventually, I will have to take my family back to claim what is rightfully ours. The search for my father continues. Jameria's been reading my mother's personal journals and have some ideas that might be a good lead. In the meantime, Houma, Louisiana is our home. And telling by the relaxed look in Liam's eyes, it's sure to be his home, too.

Acknowledgments

I want to start off by thanking God. Because without him I wouldn't be here. Next, I want to thank all those who said I wouldn't make it. Because of you I strive harder.

Now, my family. The best way to describe them is open minded and uninhibited. My true and always loyal fans. My sisters and brother, especially. You've given me so much and I thank God every day for giving me the best siblings in the world.

To my husband, the unexpected adventures, the unique experiences, and your uncanny wild side is why I'm writing today. Thank you. I love you and appreciate you.

My uncles. My mom's brothers. One isn't with us anymore, physically, but the love I feel for him in my heart is still the same. Watching my uncles as I grew up was the most amazing thing in my young life. Especially my mom's younger brother.

I remember when I was around ten or eleven when he was in a very bad accident. He was young, still living in my grandparents' house. I remember the women calling and coming by to see him. One even bought him a big color TV with a remote control (that was the shit in the early eighties). So, I stop watching the women and started paying attention to my uncles.

I learned it was their charm and how they carried themselves with that die-hard country boy style. How they would get up five days a week to make a living and never complain about it. Then watching them transform from rugged country boys to southern gentlemen. They will forever be in my heart.

 More thanks to my best friend who is more of a sister to me than a friend. You are the realist person I know. Our conversation keeps me on the right track even when I didn't know I was wandering off the straight line.

    Mom you've had some hard times. But I hope the accomplishments your children and grandchildren have made and trying to make will give you something to look forward to in the future. A single mother who raised five kids. All of them made it out of high school and three graduated from college. One graduated Cum-Lau and the other got her masters. Grab you a platinum, relax a little bit and glorify in the fact that you did a damn good job. Luv u mom.

21944129R00167

Printed in Great Britain
by Amazon